THE
NORTHERN
WINDS

IAN ANTHONY RANDALL

authorHOUSE®

AuthorHouse™
1663 Liberty Drive
Bloomington, IN 47403
www.authorhouse.com
Phone: 1 (800) 839-8640

Published by AuthorHouse 04/23/2018

ISBN: 978-1-5462-3966-6 (sc)
ISBN: 978-1-5462-3964-2 (hc)
ISBN: 978-1-5462-3965-9 (e)

Library of Congress Control Number: 2018905012

Print information available on the last page.

CONTENTS

Dedicated to Caro,
Más buena que el pan

---•◉•---

"'I have done that,' says my memory. 'I cannot have done that,'
says my pride, and remains adamant. At last—memory yields."
~ Nietzsche, *Beyond Good and Evil*

Author's Note

In Chile, the northern winds are winds blowing north to south that portend an approaching storm. In the south of Chile, the winds are said to be norteando.

PART I

SHELL BEACH, CALIFORNIA: PRESENT DAY

"We know so much of wanting, and so little of having."

The priest looks out over a quiet ocean as he speaks. We're standing on the back portico of this seaside chapel and admiring the swirling pastels of dusk. The sun is setting in the distance, a crimson thread lining a placid sky.

"How do you overcome it?" I ask. "You've given up so much for this life. How do you keep from wanting more?"

He hesitates for a moment, then answers softly. "I don't. I want what I don't have, too."

"We have so much, but it's never enough," he continues. "We're all such predictable fools."

The young priest is too wise, and too sad, for his age. He reminds me of myself when I was a young man.

"I need to be on my way. Thank you, Father." I pick up my briefcase and walk toward the front gates. As I cross the vestibule and step into the dusk, his voice carries over the empty pews.

"God bless you."

I arrive home to a silent house. My wife, Hope, is visiting our oldest son's family and won't be back until late. I pour myself a drink—Dewar's on the rocks, my usual—and step onto the back porch. The night is dim and murky, and I can't help but think back to other lonely nights in my life:

The wide-open emptiness of Patagonia, where the stars were a million fireflies that illuminated the sky.

The slothful nights of Vietnam, where the jungle's creaks and whines drove you insane with fear, and made you realize there was good reason to be afraid.

A cold and violent night in Santiago, when a city was attacked from within, and the echoing gunfire nearly drowned out the cries of children.

And now, these languid nights on the California coast, part of this picturesque life that Hope and I have built. These nights are spent surveying an endless sea and seeing the faces of those left behind in the expansive darkness. There is no darkness like the open sea, where there are no beginnings and no endings. Only the steady lapping of the waves, forever.

I am sleeping, I think, but then I am thrashing, fighting an invisible enemy that is attacking me. I'm fighting for my life as Charlie's rough hands squeeze my throat, his cold feline eyes looking straight into mine.

I open my eyes. I feel the soft linen of bed sheets. I hear the gentle rustle of the waves.

And then I see Hope's terrified eyes, consumed with fear. Somehow, my hands have encircled her throat. She is crying and gagging. She is praying to God that I wake up. I let go of her neck and wrap my arms around her.

"*Mi amor,* I'm so sorry," I say, frantically hugging her, trying to undo what I've just done. "I'm so sorry. *Te amo tanto. Te amo tanto.*" I'm saying it over and over again, chanting it like a mantra.

"Please forgive me," I finally say. Then I am quiet. We embrace like that for a while, rocking and holding each other tightly, knowing that words won't suffice. After a while she rests my head on her lap and strokes my thinning hair. I am crying softly, embarrassed but unable to hold back the tears.

When we finally lie down, we settle into contoured sides of the bed that have been molded after so many years together. We close our eyes. And then we reach out in the middle of the bed for the other's hand, as we've done so many thousands of nights before, a simple yet sacred ritual in this marriage. In the middle of the thundering stillness and the fear, we are still together. We cling to each other's hands. Hope falls back asleep and the rhythm of her breathing is calming, hypnotic.

But I still see their faces. My best friend. My twin brother. My mother. The woman I loved, before I was granted this unearned second act. I see their faces, and I know there will be no rest tonight.

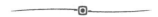

Early morning is my favorite part of the day. I wake at the first whisper of daybreak, programmed to rise as the dawn begins its gentle bow over the Pacific. The morning chill is an old companion and together we press on, achy and arthritic, determined to overcome whatever may have passed in previous days and nights. Even for an old man with a patchwork of years to his name, this forgetting of the past is never-ending, a continual work in progress.

Early morning is also when my shoulder hurts the most. The pain is a dull and far-off emptiness, as if the bullet that ripped through it so many years ago left a permanent hole. In one side and clean out the other, a telescope tunnel that never got filled. Doctors tell me that it has long since filled up with scar tissue, but my body has never accepted the replacement parts—whatever filled the wound has been found wanting, intolerably fragile and damaged. It hurts most in the early morning, when all is silent, and again at night when the quiet returns.

Winding around the north side of our home is a rocky path that crests into a seaside cliff. Diving down the cliff is a billowing sand dune that slopes gracefully to the ocean and then disappears into the willowy fingers of the lapsing waves. Every day on my morning run I trek up the winding path to the cliff, enjoying a moment of shade underneath a grove of quaking aspens, and then catapult myself down the steep dune. As I run, my legs churn as fast as a fat old man's legs can to stay underneath the tumbling belly leading the way. And always, always, as sure as the morning sun will rise, a sprawling flock of seagulls awaits me. Without fail they are halfway down the dune, clucking and pecking and revealing no intention of ceding passage.

I know they see me. I know because each and every one of them cranes their neck and stares at me with beady eyes, marveling at the crazy old man hurtling at them. But of course, they don't move right away. They don't even move when I'm halfway down the dune and I'm sure that I'm going to slam into a wall of feathers and flapping wings. No, they just sit and watch, amused by the spectacle. Only when I am mere steps away from trampling some poor stupid seagull do they flee, the entire squawking flock lumbering upward to dodge the collision and then casting accusatory glances as I pass.

They do see me. They just don't understand the danger from afar, even if it should be as obvious to them as it is to me. With all my years, maybe I'm expecting too much. It wasn't always obvious to me.

For three wide- and wild-eyed young men who were sent to fight for their adopted country in 1971, we could see the most obvious dangers in our path. And for the most part, we managed to escape them. But the rest—I never imagined what would come next. Should I have steered us away from the perils beneath the surface and between the lines that maybe weren't as unknowable as I now tell myself? Should I have known that after fighting in Vietnam, going back home to Chile was just too simple? Too poetic? Maybe we had no way of seeing the danger ahead. Or maybe we saw it coming and just didn't know how to get out of the way.

There's a sweet old Vietnamese woman named Phuong who owns a liquor store near the beach—a store that I visit more often than I care to admit. Phuong always greets me with a smile and a hearty, *Good morning, Mr. Piñera*. Per our routine, I kindly ask that she call me my Christian name, Benjamin, and she bows and politely declines. After selecting a few bottles of Dewar's from the shelves, I approach the register and initiate a familiar repartee, childish and circuitous but oh-so-dearly important.

Phuong patiently endures my small talk, inanities about the traffic and the tourists and (God help me) the weather, while I muster the courage to broach a subject I have raised with her many times before. One that has haunted me for a lifetime, an old siren over which this docile grandma with kind wrinkles holds the singular power to silence.

How are the people in Vietnam? I ask. *Are they doing better? Are the people still so poor that they only eat a bowl of rice a day, if they eat anything at all? Do they still hate each other, the North and the South?*

I haven't told her that I fought in the war, but I suspect she knows. My questioning is too needy, too desperate, to be simple chitchat. But she's the only person I can talk to about this. She gracefully parries my bashful interrogation, cataloguing the blur of questions, and then responds slowly, softly.

Phuong still has family in Vietnam, and she tells me it's getting better. *More tourists, more factories, more money,* she says. *Still poor, but not so poor,* she counsels. *North and South do not hate so much.*

And then, always, my final question: *Do they still hate us, the Americans? Do they hate the soldiers who fought there?*

Phuong concludes our chats tactfully, her deep brown eyes looking straight into mine. *No, Mr. Piñera, they don't hate the American soldiers. You were just boys. They hated the war. But everyone hates war.*

Thank you, I say, my response woefully insufficient. For her patience. For her understanding. For her maternal intuition and compassion, and a more noble spirit than I could ever hope for. I leave the tiny liquor store assuaged for a day or two, until the past again resurfaces and the wreckage pops back up like a buoy submerged in the sea.

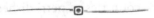

Vietnam, 1971. The mere mention of the time and place is incendiary, a jackknife dive into a dark period in American history and an even darker one for the people actually in Vietnam. If only I wasn't afflicted with this compulsion to revisit history. If only I could leave Well Enough Alone.

But it's a chapter of my life that won't go away, a time that changed everything during the war, and after, and then forever. Even with all my discarding of the past, these are the things that I can't forget, and I must stop this charade, stop acting like I was never there and never saw and heard and did what was seen and heard and done. In moments of weakness, or in the presence of inescapable nostalgia—the smell of pho, the smoky aroma of burning fields, the pungent oily musk of Napalm— the sights and sounds come flooding back to me. What's different from all my other memories, though, is that I have managed to excise myself from these.

I see the Squadron on patrol, duck walking through the emerald jungle with Cody on point and my brother JC as slack man. Just like it always was, because Cody and JC volunteering to lead was not a request but a statement of fact. I see White bringing up the rear, the whites of his eyes shining with hair-trigger alertness. I see the rest of the Squadron—O'Hare, Sanchez, Van Atta, Esposito, White, Whitaker, Johnson, Freeman— moving together like a wolf pack, wary and silent.

But I'm nowhere in the panorama. What deft trickery, what sleight of hand, to write myself out of the act. I'm off stage and behind the curtain, nowhere to be found. It's what allows me to stand on my wide weatherproofed deck and tell myself that somehow I deserved to make it out.

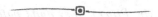

We westerners are constantly re-engineering our lives. We spin in a never-ending optimization model, exchanging variables and switching inputs like little boys trading baseball cards. Careers, houses, faces, stomachs, hair—anything that can be enhanced, augmented, refined. Bettered.

It's an addiction, this race for best, an angst largely unknown in less prosperous lives. We have the luxury to be discontent, and to want more. We have the luxury to use countries as petri dishes, betting on the end of history and then observing the reaction from afar.

The Vietnamese? They crouch on their haunches in the smog-enshrouded streets and banter, smiling only when it's unavoidable, while their women vend trinkets and steer naked children clear of passing scooters. They sort through misfortunes like menial tasks and prioritize, relegating lesser mishaps to the bottom of the list to leave space for more pressing setbacks and prominent sorrows. There are few why's, or how's. There simply Is, What Was and What Will Be, and a stoic acquiescence to that reality.

All the talk of Communism and Capitalism, the theorizing of powerful men in underground bunkers and ivory towers, was as fictitious to them as a fairy tale. It would have been harmless, as well, if it weren't for the ensuing war that led millions of men, women and children to kill each other in all sorts of ways, from the mundane to the grotesque. Everyone killed everyone. No one was innocent, least of all the Viet Cong, who slaughtered hundreds of thousands of South Vietnamese in cold blood after they captured Saigon.

If it had only been Vietnam, it would be easier to leave behind. It would be a vague remembrance; a nightmare, to be sure, but one that faded with time. But it was not so simple. There was only one escape and it was to the land of our birth, where our ancestors carved out a sparse existence beneath the glowering peaks of the Andes. In the end, Chile was entangled in the same sprawling web as Vietnam, fighting the same battle engineered from afar. The rub is that we could never escape, not even in Chile. Not anywhere. Our realities are so much bigger than ourselves. We control our own lives, no more, and rely on the grace of God and the arrested humanity of others for the rest. And sometimes, they fail us.

This is not a story about the Vietnam War. Not really, anyway, at least not the kind that digs down into the black heart of war and pulls out something meaningful, because I can't tell poignant war stories. I tell them anyway, unable to bury the impulse to purge these jagged fragments, but I'm still unable to make sense of it. I'm as ignorant today as I was then about the reasons men are sent to kill other men, women and children, and about how to explain it. I just know it was fear, and adrenaline, and loneliness, and madness, and blood and guts and bitterness and hatred, and brotherhood. And loss. A lot of loss, of losing more than you ever knew you had to lose. I know that it's instinctual, the putting of words to what we see and hear, but it's eternally insufficient. And I know the words don't change anything. Maybe they help you remember, and the spirits awaken for a time, but they don't change anything.

It all starts with Vietnam, you could say, but then it fades back to where it really started, in a land at war with itself that nobody noticed. And it ends up in the California Hills, somewhere among the restless secrets of an old man. Or rather, it starts decades ago on a rainy night in that land that nobody noticed, a dark rainy night beneath the Andes when everything changed and twin-faced boys lost everything for the first time. And it never ends.

How do you explain the things that you've done? That you've lied and cheated, and that you've hurt others. That you've left good men behind. That you've killed. That you have failed, over and over again, to be the eyes and ears and hands of God. How does anyone burden that weight? It wasn't your fault, you tell yourself. You were a kid, sent to a war you didn't start. You did your job. And you did what you were *really* supposed to do, which was survive. But where does it fit in this life of an aging immigrant grandpa who can't forget what he is supposed to? Questions without answers. Fragments that detonate inside my head and embed themselves even deeper.

There is no easy way to talk about those years. This life of mine is scattered, made of parts that don't fit together the way they are supposed to, and the whole story makes even less sense in its entirety. There's nothing I can do to change that, to make this compilation less clumsy or add levity. The few good things, I have tried to hang onto, and I'll tell you about some of those, too. But it will be hard to make this coherent, to make it polished and logical. To relay events in chronological order, as if recounting a summer vacation from yesteryear, would only lend a mask of rationality to a time when nothing made sense. Doing so would forsake these memories, ignore that they are living—that they are dancing skeletons that rattle and shake in waking life. They remind and reminisce every second of every day.

Silence is not exculpatory no matter how much we wish it to be. The years go by and we hope they consign the past to another time, when we were someone else, or at least a different version of ourselves. But we are who we are Who We Are. Yesterday was yesterday, and today is today. The chapter, the verse: That which has been done, is that which will be done. There is no new thing under the sun.

Through it all I've been lying to myself. This great illusion, this deletion of my own presence, is actually a scam wherein I'm the perpetrator and the victim. I forget, but the skeletons dance on into the night. And in this hazy half-remembrance, I lose all that remained of Cody and Juan Carlos, and Suyai, and my once-beloved Ayelen, and of the blessed people who took us in and tried to protect us after the not-quite war was not quite over. I can't lose them, not again.

PART II

VIETNAM: 1971

I swiveled the M-16 rifle around the corner of the thatched-roof hut. On the far side of the hut, a Viet Cong soldier was bending down to pick up his rifle from the ground. The Viet Cong guerilla held the weapon in one hand with a tenuous grip on the barrel of the rifle. Just ten feet behind him, an American soldier had been shot in the stomach. This particular soldier had died trying to put his insides back inside.

I immediately knew he was Charlie: the glistening AK-47, the conical rice hat, the black VC pajama shirt covered with pockets, the munitions strapped to a woven belt and provisions packed into a cloth bandolier slung around his shoulder. A beige rice bag hung limply to his side like a deflated balloon, and rice poured slowly out of a hole in the bottom of the bag. His once-white sandals were stained a deep red and caked with mud. Straightening his back, the slight man looked squarely into my eyes, silent and unmoving.

I pinpointed his chest in my rifle sights. He dropped the rifle and hung his arms to the side, as if to say, *What else can I do?*

I fired the rifle. One more bullet exploded from one more gun barrel. One more bullet in a fusillade of firefights and grenades and projectile mines and scorched-earth bombings.

The VC soldier's head jerked back violently. The man staggered for a moment like a dazed boxer and then fell forward onto his face. His chin struck the ground and bounced back up off the muddy soil with grotesque force. The only sound I heard was a muted gasp, and then a soft expulsion of breath. In his final moments, the man writhed for a solitary moment, his neck craning back in an attempt to pull his face out of the streaming rivulets of reddish-brown water. Then he lay still. On the left side of his back a small crimson dot appeared, growing outward in mottled concentric circles and staining the black cloth of his uniform.

The rain continued to fall. Overhead, the monkeys howled their incessant chants, blood-curdling screams originating from a dark and unknowable depth. Behind me, my twin brother Juan Carlos appeared, panting and soaked to the bone.

"We need to get out of here. Charlie is everywhere and it's going to be hot. Cody said the Sergeant heard reports of a Viet Cong Battalion headed this way." In the distance, a Huey was landing and American soldiers were grabbing any inch of metal available for the dust-off.

"He was looking me in the eyes when I shot him."

"That's not the first VC you've killed."

"But he was looking me in the eyes when I shot him."

JC shook his head. "Fuck it. We need to go. The airlift is leaving."

A clear view of the Huey's landing zone was impeded by the busty canopy. Jackfruit, strangler fig and mangrove trees sidled upward in the disjointed swamps and rice paddies, trunks gnarly and black, their bright green leaves garish in the presence of the surrounding death fields. Boroughs of unctuous gray smoke trawled upwards into the sky. The air was putrid, the smell of singed human skin and hair mixing with the subtle sweetness of the rice fields and the fishy garlic of the villagers' morning pho breakfast. A child bleated in the distance, the obstinate chorus line of Vietnam. And the awesome concerto played on: the chopper blades laying a laconic baseline; the rat-a-tat-tat of machine gun fire issuing snare drum blasts; the crackles of the burning homes sending the strings into a violent crescendo; and once gone, a coda of silence and finality.

It had been at least a full day since we had slept and every step moved a mountain. Bone-tired and blurry eyed, JC and I ran toward the distant thumping of the chopper blades. To my right, a flash of black sprang up out of the brush like a jack-in-the-box. A machine gun burst fired behind me. As I dove to take cover, I saw a black-clad VC soldier collapse, blood spewing from his wounds. The soldier's rifle fell harmlessly to the ground. When I stood up I saw Private Johnson with his rifle raised, smoke trawling from its barrel.

"I just saved your Mexican ass."

"I'm Chilean, motherfucker."

"Let's didi out of here."

I turned and took a step forward, listening for the whooshing sound of the dust-off to orient myself.

The force of the blow catapulted me forward on my stomach like an insect skimming across a pond. Everything was still. The only reason I knew I was alive was because of the sting in my eyes from the mud and grit. Johnson was dead, ripped Through & Through by a Bouncing Betty mine most likely stolen from one of the South Vietnamese Army's supply convoys. I cast a perfunctory look back at the carnage. Johnson was in at least three pieces.

JC pulled me up off the ground. "He's gone. Let's go."

We reached the Air Cav landing zone, grabbed onto the hovering Huey's foot bars and pulled ourselves up to the helicopter. The smoke was a plastic film pulled taut over our faces. The chopper banked and boogied south and the village became a distant ember, one more red-hot coal in the raging inferno of Vietnam that had taken the best years of our lives, and in the end would surely take all of it.

Later on that night I lay awake in my tent listening to soldiers' futile attempts to sleep. On any given night the rustling sounds of grunts desperate for sleep or whimpering from too-vivid nightmares could be heard in all directions, competing for the dense night space with caroling mosquitoes and screeching beetles. As I lay on my back and adjusted the itchy plastic poncho to block strands of rainwater pouring in through the seams, the rain outside fell in fat plunks, pelting the roof of the tent. The rain would come down all night and wash away the day's newly spilled blood. But it would never be enough to cleanse the land.

My father, JC and I lived through a surreal year in California before JC and I were drafted and sent to Vietnam. Our family lived in Chile until 1970, but fled to California to get away from the brewing Chilean civil war. And for a while, life seemed to resume some semblance of reality. But we were blinded by our do-over life in California, and we never saw Vietnam coming.

JC and I received the order to report for medical exams in early spring; our draft cards arrived shortly thereafter. One day we were riding the bus to school and screwing up phrasal verbs, and the next we were reporting for Army physicals. We had been in the States less than a year, working as bus boys at a local restaurant and nearing high school graduation. By summer we were headed to Basic Training, an ancillary benefit of naturalized citizenship.

There was always the possibility of a deferment if we went to college, but we were still struggling with the language and barely passing classes. And with Father still unemployed, we could hardly pay the rent. There just wasn't any spare money to send two kids to college, especially two quasi-fluent immigrants. Further complicating matters, Nixon signed an Executive Order in '70 limiting deferments. In this new world, we were definitely not the best and the brightest, and we were sent to fight.

Cody always knew he would join the military and enlisted before we even graduated from high school. It was always expected that the Pollard men would serve their country: Cody's dad had been a grunt in WWII, he proudly told us, and his grandfather served in the Great War. A self-admitted redneck with a linebacker's frame and a soldier's flat top, Cody was the toughest kid I had ever met, not scared of anything or anybody. His family lived in the dusty inland valleys near Bakersfield, sharing the open skies with farmers and migrant workers. The wealthier coastal kids often called those from the valley Bakos, but only JC and I could say it to his face. We didn't say it hurtfully, and he knew that we too were outcasts, even more so than him. I still don't know how we became such good friends during that year in California. Because he enlisted when we got our induction letters, we all headed to Fort Ord in Monterrey for Basic at the same time. Scared as JC and I were, we were lucky enough to be deployed together, with Cody at our side. Most draftees didn't have that luxury.

———————◉———————

I had to go to the other side of the world to learn real fear. The fear that I learned there, that visceral gut-deep fear, was unlike anything I had ever known.

Arriving to base camp in Vietnam, the first days and nights were engulfed by fear, and not knowing what to be afraid of: a guerilla ambush, a grenade launched from the bush by the enemy or a disgruntled grunt looking to frag an officer, the infamous Bouncing Betty land mines that shredded men into confetti, or the razor sharp bamboo stakes sheathed in pit traps and smeared with feces to cause infection. Even the relatively pedestrian fears like poisonous snakes hiding in the backwoods or a nasty case of VD from choosing the wrong *me love you long time* girl weighed on soldiers. New Privates took that fateful first step off the Hercules C-130 cargo planes and were met by the primal scent of bloodlust.

I never doubted that my fellow soldiers felt the same way. Fear is palpable, and fear is contagious. We quickly realized that the only thing standing between Charlie and us was our Platoon and our Squadron. While the Army was not immune from the battles being fought back home—black and white, poor and middle-class, and hip and square were all shipped over to Vietnam as baby-faced GIs—the divisions became subordinate to battlefield loyalty because we all wanted to stay alive. In time, though, I learned that war can make an enemy out of everyone, even those wearing the same uniform.

On the first night in the barracks after lights out, we lay sweating on the nylon mattresses and wondered what surprises awaited us outside camp. Private White, a quiet lumbering kid from Detroit, leaned on his elbow and tapped my shoulder.

"Does Charlie usually attack at night?"

"Who knows. Maybe. This camp has a good perimeter defense, though. Did you see the old Dusters on the perimeter? Each one has an M-60 mounted in back."

"Yeah, man, I saw the Guns," he said. "But what happens if they sneak through the perimeter?"

It was hard not to imagine what would happen if they broke through—Charlie with a knife at our throats before we ever woke up.

"It won't happen." I didn't really believe my own words. "But if you hear anything, wake me up. I'll do the same for you."

15

"It's a deal," he said. My first alliance against the fear.

-------◉-------

We arrived in the heart of the '71 rainy season alongside dozens of other newly minted Privates assigned to the 1ˢᵗ Air Cavalry Division. Many more soldiers were headed the opposite way: *rotating*, as it was called, returning to a country not quite ready to pardon their service. Other returning GIs wouldn't suffer the indignity of being spat on and jeered at. They arrived solemnly, out of the public eye, with shiny American flags folded over their chests in crisp triangles.

Tan Nhut Air Force base, the major hub in Vietnam for arriving and departing military personnel, was bustling with troop movements and aircraft traffic. After the C-130 dropped us off on the tarmac, we crossed in front of a Chinook landing on an adjacent airstrip. The groan of its circulating blades eclipsed all peripheral sound, subordinating the landing area to the powerful machine. There were soldiers everywhere, thousands upon thousands of soldiers.

The base was a fortified concrete structure encircled by bunkers and control towers. As we neared the base, an F-4 Phantom rocketed overhead and left a thin white trail that parted the overcast sky. I looked back and saw Cody shouting something in JC's ear and pointing toward the Chinook. Both Cody and JC stopped dead in their tracks, still and transfixed, staring at the colossal transport helicopter. As the swarm of new soldiers was shooed off the tarmac and into a high-roofed hangar, I turned and walked toward JC and Cody to hurry them along. When Cody saw me approaching he waved me away but I continued anyway.

"Guys, what the hell are you looking at? We have to follow the Sergeant."

My eyes scanned across the tarmac, an open field littered with supply crates and camouflage Jeeps, and finally settled on the Chinook. A group of soldiers rolled large dollies across a grass field toward the aircraft. Each shelf of the metallic gray carts held a row of black leather bags with shiny silver zippers, all zipped up tight, that jostled as they rolled across the bumpy field. Behind the Chinook, empty coffins had been aligned in neat rows, their covers resting against the smooth wooden boxes like miniature lean-to's. Military Police officers stood by the coffins wearing black gloves and holding American flags tightly under their arms. The dollies clanked along the bumpy tarmac, and the MPs stared straight ahead with somber expressions, looking at nothing and seeing no one.

Ahead, an officer yelled at us from the hangar, angrily waving his arms. We shouldered our rucksacks and ran to catch up to the new crop of grunts.

Lifers and short timers called newly arriving privates "cherries", if they deigned to talk to us at all. The graphic metaphor was not lost on us. Nagging doubts about our readiness were as constant as officers barking orders in our ears, doubts that no amount of training would pacify. But the Cav had suffered heavy losses in the past year, especially in the '70 Cambodia campaign and the '71 Laos debacle, and they needed more Airbornes for their particularly hazardous brand of combat. We were the fresh meat, the *Fucking New Guys*. As FNGs, we kept our mouths shut and obeyed orders.

The Cav was one of the fiercest and most battle-tested divisions in the Army. Vietnamese operations dated back to the Pleiku campaign in '65, making it one of the longest-standing American divisions in the war. Since its arrival, the Cav had supplied the central highlands and III Corps around Saigon with their primary firepower: boots on the ground, Airborne troopers, and advanced search-and-destroy and mobile artillery capabilities. The Cav took a twisted pride in having suffered so many casualties, a sentiment that was hard to miss, even as FNGs. No matter how thick the shit, the Cav went in and cleared ground. They kept sending us in because we did our job no matter the cost.

In war there is no normal day, but most days did include long stretches of boredom: the waiting, the warring with teeming insects and the bouts of malarial sweating. These rituals were interrupted by patrols tracking Charlie along the maze of dirt paths that wound from the Demilitarized Zone to Saigon. These patrols often turned up nothing, amounting to a grueling slog through hot and rancid jungles, with insects as big as snakes and snakes as big as people.

When we did see combat, it usually came after Charlie ambushed a patrol in the field. The initial damage they inflicted started a race against time, pitting how many men they could take down in the opening salvo against how many we could kill with artillery and air strikes. We had precious few moments to call in F-15s and Skyhawk helicopters before Charlie disappeared back into their jungle lair. These guerillas would only be seen again when they next attacked, or in the vaguely reminiscent faces we passed on village patrols after they melted back into the civilian population. I quickly learned that winning and killing more of the enemy than they kill of you are two very different things. Especially when you're not sure who it is you're killing. South Vietnam had about 20 million people in 1971. At one time or another it seemed like every one of them popped out of the bush wielding a Kalashnikov.

In my first few combat missions I was confounded by the task of telling friend from foe. Short of requiring sympathetic South Vietnamese to wear an insignia on their clothes, there was no reliable way to know who your enemy was until you were looking down the barrel of a gun. I could still recall my first mission, when my squad had terminated two targets and taken a third POW.

We were escaping through the south end of village in the soft light of dawn, serrated K-Bar knives firmly affixed to the POW's spine. To the east, a man dressed in dark clothing stepped out from underneath a bough of low-hanging jackfruit trees. A white cloth was wrapped loosely around his thin torso. In his hands he held something dark, but the man and the object were blurry and indistinguishable given the distance and the glare of the rising sun. I raised my rifle and scanned the field for more VC, and saw nothing.

All three soldiers in my squad fired simultaneously. The man collapsed into the tall elephant grass. Was he another VC guerrilla disguised as a civilian? Or a peasant farmer tending his crops at sunrise?

PFC Freeman, a skinny black kid from southern Alabama, later explained the actual rules of engagement to me.

"You see a local, and you're not sure—you shoot him, or her. I lost my best friend because he was trying to figure out whether a ten year-old girl was Charlie. She shot him between the eyes."

That was the first and last tutorial I would receive. I swear to God I didn't want to kill civilians. But I didn't want to die, either.

At first, covert operations were conducted in the early morning hours, quick-strike raids on high-value VC targets identified by Phoenix, the Army's intelligence unit. Combat units put their lives on the line based on their Intel, moving into hostile territory using information gleaned (or extracted) from VC guerillas or reconnaissance missions. We just hoped they had it right.

As time went on and Charlie came to expect interdiction raids, it was harder to enter covertly into any forward operating area. In later years, Special Ops units were usually led by a Kit Carson scout, a former VC guerrilla or sympathizer who played Judas for an extra bundle of dong, or because Charlie couldn't pay his monthly wage. These were not men to be trusted, but they were better than going in blind and walking straight into a VC Battalion.

From our post in Loc Ninh, a base northwest of Saigon near the Cambodian border, our unit was ideally positioned to sweep east into the Iron Triangle, a hotbed of VC resistance. Early in the war, much of the covert action occurred in this area between the Thi-Tinh and Saigon rivers, a land of boundless rice paddies and wary peasant farmers. This traditional VC stronghold was made all the more lethal by Charlie's complex system of underground tunnels centered around Cu Chi, a subterranean maze spanning thousands of miles. American operations in '67 and '68 were unsuccessful in disabling the underground tunnel system, with bombing campaigns, bulldozers, and flooding all proving futile. Even specially trained "tunnel rats" entering with only a flashlight and a handgun failed to dislodge them from their shadowy labyrinths.

Missions in the Iron Triangle intensified in July, when Cody, JC and I first began to join the Special Ops teams conducting the raids. As Phoenix came to understand the strategic relevance of coordination between the Viet Cong and the North Vietnamese Army, the capture of key VC leaders became even more critical.

That was also when our Platoon began to conduct secret raids in Cambodia.

O'Hare insisted on polishing his boots every night. Although our packs were already weighed down by an assortment of gadgets intended to keep us alive, he had dutifully schlepped a full shoeshine kit since arriving in Saigon. It didn't matter that the only polish available in Vietnam was a tarry black goo that was an entirely different color than the Army's standard-issue jungle boots and made him look like he'd sunk ankle deep into quicksand. He still kept shining them, night after night.

There was something rhythmic and quieting about the midnight routine: the patient scrubbing of worn leather with the buffing brush, the application of a fresh layer to conceal the stains and gashes, and the final cleaning with a white rag stained black from use. The discolored shine was short lived, though. As soon as he stepped outside of his tent and back into the muck, any sign of the previous night's labor was scraped off and washed away.

You know that shit is not going to stay on, we told him.

He just nodded. *I know, I know.* But he kept on polishing, all the same.

We gave O'Hare a hard time about it, but we were all guilty of clinging to our own rituals. Cody had his morning push-ups and sit-ups, sixty of each as dependable as clockwork, and JC his aimless nighttime walks circling whatever jerry-rigged perimeter had been set. I had mine too, red herrings that let me pretend I was still in control of the hours of the day.

The Bible was pocket sized, with print so small I had to squint to read it. Lights out snuck up on us most nights so I often resorted to dipping underneath my blanket with a dimmed flashlight to read a few pages before bed. As a boy, I was enchanted by the poignancy of Ecclesiastes, the lyricism of Psalms and the righteous fury of Jeremiah, and in spite of my waning faith I returned to those worn pages for solace. But I never told anyone I read the Bible or even that I carried it with me. Therein was a memory, one of a mother's lullaby voice, that was mine alone.

The other routine was walking to the market to buy fresh fruit. Outside of most combat bases there were rows of vendors hawking produce from the local fields. The markups were outlandish, with prices four times what the locals paid, but the routine of strolling through the fruit stands like just another afternoon shopper was comforting.

After spending a few months at Loc Ninh I developed a go-to kiosk. She was an elderly woman missing most of her teeth who always greeted me warmly. Her English was limited, almost as bad as my Vietnamese, but we managed to communicate through animated pointing, finger counting and smiling. After our signed bantering, a final thumbs up signified an agreement had been reached.

Despite her limited language, she was harmlessly coquettish with me. *Such a handsome boy*, she would say. She made a sincere effort to help me pick out the freshest fruit and charged a reasonable GI markup. More importantly, she never tried to deceive me like the others did, with their slapdash tricks to unload rotten fruit on otherwise preoccupied soldiers.

One day, I remember well. It was a cloudy afternoon, a day when Charlie was on the doorstep and we were waiting for the mortars to start howling. I rushed to the stand and hastily grabbed a bunch of small bananas and a handful of fruits that looked like oblong oranges. I asked her the price and she began counting the bananas. When she looked at the tangerine fruits, she waved her hand in disapproval.

"No. Don't want this."

"Why not?"

"Not good. I help." I wondered if my urgency had gone unnoticed. Or did she know something I didn't and was trying to stall my return to the base? It wouldn't have been the first time a seemingly harmless local aided a VC attack.

She scooted around the cart and began squeezing the fruits. After carefully scrutinizing them, she placed the ones I had chosen back onto the pile and tossed new ones into a paper bag.

"Only these are ready to eat."

"Why? I don't understand."

"Bitter," she said, the word exploding from her mouth with unabashed pride. Her English was actually much better than my Vietnamese. "Very bitter. Want sweet."

"So these are better?"

"Yes, much better. But only eat up to here," she said, pointing to a yellow band on the fruit.

"Really? Up to here?"

"Yes. Only to here." She traced a line around the fruit with her finger. "No more."

"OK. I need to go."

As I jogged away from the kiosk she offered a shy wave. I wanted to trust her, but I had learned the hard way that in this war, people were often not what they seemed.

I arrived back at the base as the evening darkened. Sitting on my cot, I peeled the fruits and shoveled them in my mouth. The meat was juicy and sweet. Remembering her advice, I set the remaining pieces on the bedpost and tried to forget about the hunger gnawing at my stomach.

I waited a few minutes but the shelling still hadn't begun. Having eaten only a bowl of rice that day, I was famished, and I reexamined the remaining pieces. Although lighter in color, how different could it be from the rest? Maybe she *was* trying to stall me. I peeled one of the remaining pieces and ate it.

The fruit was inedible, a sandpapery burst of bitterness. I spit it out and rubbed my gums to purge the ghastly taste, laughing out loud at my foolishness.

In Vietnam, trust was a commodity in short supply. That I could have trusted the old woman with a crooked smile made me remember what it was like to be normal, capable of believing in the random kindness of a stranger.

The Vietnamese rainy season spanned from early May through September. For those five months you ate, drank, sweated, pissed and dreamed rain. The monsoons and cackling thunderstorms unleashed torrents so relentless and unforgiving that the rain permeated your physical borderlines, muddling the edges between where you ended and the outside wetness began.

Charlie was on the move that rainy season, funneling supplies through Laos and Cambodia and preparing for an offensive we all knew was coming. After the South Vietnamese Army's failure in Operation Lan Som, the bungled South Vietnamese-led incursion into Laos, Charlie saw weakness in their enemies: an emasculated American military that had lost support for the war back home and an ineffectual South Vietnamese force that couldn't fight its way out of a paper bag. We called the South Vietnamese Army ARVN—one more acronym tossed around to further normalize the ludicrous state of our lives. Reports of VC supply movements around the DMZ and in Laos were everywhere, and interdicting those supply routes became a top priority for the Army.

It was after ARVN's fiasco in Laos that both sides settled in for a protracted knife fight. The Viet Cong attacked like the pumas we had grown up with in the Chilean Patagonia: if they let you see them, you could be damn sure they were going to attack. When we were sent out to track VC after guerilla ambushes, the only Vietnamese we came across were rural farmers working rice paddies in some idyllic village. Of course, we knew that the Viet Cong kept peasant outfits at the ready to blend back into the civilian population after an attack. But how to know who to interrogate, who to capture. Who to kill?

Sergeant Francis Lombardi was the commanding officer of our unit, the 7th Cavalry. Lombardi was from Philly, the oldest son of a big Italian-American union family that had sparred on more than one picket line. His dad had been a union activist who escaped Italy in 1941, when the Fascists were still hunting unions and fighting alongside Hitler. They arrived at Ellis Island before Italian partisans got their revenge and hung Mussolini's lifeless remains from a meat hook in a downtown Milanese plaza. Lombardi's accent sounded like his mouth was full of marbles, and he spit out words like a machine gun, harsh and unremitting. He always told the truth and never asked his men to do something he wouldn't. Among an ocean of officers that were despised, Lombardi was respected. Revered, actually, because he cared whether we lived or died.

Lombardi was smart enough to hide his politics from the Army. Soldiers in general didn't talk politics because our opinions didn't matter one way or the other, but his past could have been a problem so he kept it close to the vest. The only reason that we ever found about it was because of his weakness for hard liquor.

Twice a year soldiers were given a weekend pass to Saigon for a little

R&R. It was hard for officers to ignore how far morale had plunged when grunts were fragging officers on a daily basis, and officers figured that any possible leave time might dial back the resentment. JC, Cody and I received the treasured passes for Thanksgiving weekend. We boarded a Chinook headed for Saigon and prepared to drink ourselves numb.

The early Friday evening was buzzing with the vitality of a big city night and enlivened by hoards of GIs roaming the streets looking to spend their hard-earned wages. Walking down Le Lai Street in Central Park we weaved between boys kicking badminton birdies back and forth. On the boardwalk, diminutive old women foisted sweet jelly treats out from underneath wide hats, their veiny hands translucent like freshly pressed rice paper. Families sat underneath sprawling trees and shared a meal, keeping a keen eye on toddlers who wandered through the crowded park walkways.

As we walked down the promenade leading to the central market, two skinny boys made of elbows and knees bounced around us with big brown eyes, wearing playful grins and offering high fives. We slapped their hands and smiled back. As we turned away, they extended upturned palms. *We play. You pay for play.* Saddened, we moved away from the scam. As we walked down the street I felt the sharp ping of a stone hit me square in the back. There was no winning with the Vietnamese people. There were only degrees of losing.

Dodging the lurching motorbikes and platform trucks that filled the road, we weaved across the boulevard. After reaching the other side, we saw Lombardi posted up at a bar adjacent to the central market. He was sitting on one of the small wooden stools that adorned so many of the Vietnamese bars, drinking a tall glass of something brown and syrupy.

Even from a block away it was clear Lombardi was drunk. His glazed cherry-red eyes and bemused smirk made clear he had been drinking for a while. As we neared the Tiki bar covered by a straw veranda, Lombardi noticed us and flung his arm out in an awkward wave. There was a brief flicker of embarrassment that crossed the Sergeant's face, but moments later he was inviting us to join and ordering beers from a nearby waiter.

"Boys, have a seat. Drinks are on me." He waved to the waiter once again, who ignored his booming voice. The teenage boy sat at the bar talking to his friend, their quacking intonations rising and falling like bugle calls.

"No thank you, sir," I said. "We're just out for some fresh air. We need to get back soon."

I knew that drinking in broad daylight wouldn't be a problem, even in a district crawling with MPs—the Army had bigger problems with soldiers strung out on heroin and addicted to coke. But drinking with our CO could be a major snafu if the wrong person passed by.

Lombardi raised his eyebrows and sized me up. "OK, suit yourself. If you boys want to play GI Joe go right ahead. But I'm going to dispense with the bullshit and enjoy my Scotch."

"Sergeant, I didn't know you frequented this part of town," Cody said. "Come to party with the grunts?"

Laughing, Cody's dimples crept up into his cheeks and he was instantly disarming. He was capable of loosening people up in a distinctly down-home American fashion, a quality that still eluded JC and me.

"I have to admit, I do come here once in a while. It's the only place in this godforsaken country where I can get a real drink, even if the ice does give me the runs." As he spoke he lifted up the bottle in a reverential salute. His voice was uncomfortably loud and his words reverberated through the din of the street. We waited to be dismissed, but he poured himself another drink and leaned back against the wall.

"So. You're *not* drinking? You boys aren't taking all of this too seriously, are you? You're not becoming lifers, like those grunts who get their jollies mutilating corpses? Don't do that. You're too good for that."

We stared at each other, calibrating a response. Finally Cody spoke up. "Sir, we are just trying to do our job and watch each other's backs."

"Goddamnit, Pollard, good answer," Lombardi shouted. "Very good answer, indeed." Lombardi returned to his drink. When he spoke again, he was much quieter.

"The Army isn't so bad, if you don't take it too seriously. For God's sake, I'm a card-carrying Socialist. Did you guys know that? An actual Commie. But I come in, do my job and forget about the rest. You understand me?"

"Kind of, sir," I said.

"The Army owns my ass, just like it owns yours. But at least everybody is poor here, and we're all in the shit together. It's a damn near perfect egalitarian society. And all the profiteering bullshit is far enough away that I can pretend it doesn't exist."

"In the end, we've all got to do something. I do this." Lombardi gulped down the rest of the tumbler and sighed.

"Just remember, boys, don't take it too seriously," he said. "This is not your life. You're dismissed."

———————◉———————

Lombardi was the first person I had known who admitted they were a Communist. When we were boys, Father didn't permit us to associate with *Marxistas,* as he called them. His distaste for them was hard to miss—even saying the word caused him to grimace and contort his mouth as if spitting out rotten meat. The funny thing was that Chile was overflowing with Communists, but as children we had no idea that they were living amongst us—like *regular people*—and that every day we passed them on the street and talked to them in stores. To the contrary, I thought of them as aliens, a belief borne of both Father's contempt and an awareness of the unassailable space between their and Father's Chile.

When we were maybe five or six, I asked JC if he thought that Communists looked like normal people, or if there was some way that we could tell them apart—different colored hair, maybe, or some other kind of physical oddity. JC didn't know one way or the other. *They're just different,* he said, shrugging his bony shoulders. A self-evident truth that was part of our tightly wound and tinted world.

Later, in California, Communism seemed just as foreign and diabolical as it did in Chile, if not more so. It was still an unknown, a blurry enemy that lurked in the shadows. Even after California became a Mecca for radicals in the early 70's, it was still hard to meet living and breathing Commies. Hippies and freaks were plentiful, but even the most free-loving Deadhead wasn't about to willingly paint themselves red. During the drudgery of the Cold War, even appearing to be a sympathizer was risky, and much worse than being counterculture. It meant you were an enemy of the state and of the boys fighting overseas.

As for Vietnam, Lombardi's political leanings were only slightly more relevant than our own. At the time it seemed paradoxical that our CO was a dyed-in-the-wool Communist, but Vietnam was a playground for paradoxes: fighting to keep the peace, winning over hearts and minds with bombs, and then handing Vietnam over to a government despised by the vast majority of Vietnamese people. In comparison, Lombardi's drunken admission was amusing, nothing more than a passing curiosity.

While Lombardi's politics mattered little to us, what scared the hell out of us was his fatalism. He didn't play well as a broken-down soldier, and seeing him a bad break away from losing it shook us. This was the man who led us into battle, upon whose decisions our disposable grunt lives depended. We would have been drinking anyway, but after that we resolved to drink ourselves into oblivion.

Wartime heightens the senses in a way that can't be turned off. To be always alert is to be constantly alarmed by dangers, real or imagined. In a certain light, anything can seem like a threat. A clumsy tuk-tuk driver who bounces up on the sidewalk becomes a stealth assassin, or a beggar child morphs into a grenade-wielding bomber. Trying to turn it off was as futile as pretending that you weren't in Vietnam. It's what becomes of a soldier. The simple pleasure of boozing with friends, that freewheeling excitement of drinking and youthful caprice, was a cruel joke from another reality. We drank like vets, grisly old men commiserating with empty bottles.

We ended up a block south of Central Park at an open-air bar on the strip. A lethargic breeze dissipated overhead, leaving behind a stuffy mélange of jasmine, fish sauce and urine. Three middle-aged Vietnamese businessmen in threadbare black suits argued loudly and smoked foul cigarettes out of ornate cigarette holders, a colonial French luxury dissonant amid the poverty. Feral dogs and small children competed for space in the nooks and crannies of the neighborhood, and prostitutes paraded up and down the street like peacocks, crowing half-heartedly into the crowds. *Boom-Boom? Boom-Boom?* We struggled to avoid eye contact with them, although deprived libidos drew our gazes to other body parts.

Within a minute nine shots of rice wine disappeared from our wobbly plastic table. The Vietnamese businessmen took note of the purposeful young GIs. The nerves still weren't quiet, so we ordered nine more. They went down faster than the first rounds. Then we started drinking.

After a few hours of sucking down lukewarm beers and tangy shots of rice wine, the alcohol burrowed further down and a warm mistiness subdued my wits. As I began to close my eyes, Cody's booming voice jolted me awake, back to the dingy bar and the begging children and the phalanx of scooters darting through the monolithic masses.

"So how in the fuck do we meet some women here?"

"Good luck, brother. The only women you're getting here are bought and paid for," JC said.

"It's a goddamned sad state of affairs, boys," Cody said. "I bet all those draft-dodging college boys back home are getting laid right now."

"FUBAR," JC said, bringing the first real laugh of the night.

"FUBAR," we all repeated in unison, and clinked our bottles together. Fucked Up Beyond All Recognition sounded about right.

A few minutes of soft, silent inebriation passed. I stared at the sky and searched for the stars through the city smog.

Cody awoke from his trance. "So what are we going to do about it?" The redneck Bako accent was thickest when he was drunk.

As if on cue, two smoky Vietnamese girls walked by, with button noses, small shoulders and lithe figures.

"Hey darling," Cody yelled, loud enough for the entire block to hear.

They turned slowly toward the table. Cody grinned deliriously, his drunken eyes trailing her like a sprinkler head.

"Hello," she said meekly.

"You girls want to join us?" Cody asked, his face lighting up.

They looked at each other, giggled and exchanged rapid fire Vietnamese. One of them seemed to nod.

The taller one with soft black hair cascading down her back took the initiative. "OK. But we get friend first. She speaks English best. And she is prettiest."

This was too good to be true. We looked at each other, hardly believing our luck. Three beautiful Vietnamese girls who weren't pros were coming to have drinks with us. We nervously slammed our beers and ordered six more for the group. The girls were returning and their friend was truly a knockout, a gorgeous dove of a woman with cute dimples and great curves.

"Hello boys," the new girl said.

"*Xin chào*," JC said, replying in kind. "Have a seat."

The three girls delicately lowered themselves onto the sagging picnic chairs and sipped their beers. All three of us blurted out questions at the same time, an unintelligible stream of maladroit testosterone.

Where are you from/Where do you work/Do you date Americans?

They shared another sideways glance and giggled.

"Yes. We like Americans. You are very handsome boys."

Cody began to raise his glass in a toast, but then she continued, as demurely as before. "How much for date? We give good price to handsome soldiers. *Boom-Boom? Boom-Boom?*"

Silence, again. It descended like a molten ash cloud, dense and choking. We returned to our surly drinking, broiling in our foolishness, the outbreak of optimism silly in the presence of fallen angel princesses who had to sell their bodies to survive.

In the dead of night, when the reverie of dreams tells hidden truths, I awoke cloudy eyed and rolled out of bed and into the street, swirling through the dense throngs like a weightless maple seed.

Saigon is a gale of crowded, squawking, poignant humanity, unmasked and unadulterated. The slender alleyway streets decorated by clotheslines and knotted wires are ripe with the fermenting scent of leftovers tossed in shallow gutters; the winding stone paths are lined with wrinkled matrons serving watery noodle soup to bare-chested children who sit cross-legged around small wooden tables, their feet stained a dark coal color. Teenage girls work family kiosks selling fried squid hanging from fish lines, and the paper-thin seafood sways back and forth in the hot breeze. Wrinkled grandfathers with weathered skin and sinewy muscles glued to skeleton frames perch on tiny stools, wearing only white boxer shorts and rubber tire sandals, and gaze quizzically at the newest batch of foreigners in their country. The old men move little but see all as they contemplate this latest iteration of Vietnam, a country unrecognizable from that of their youth. Gap-toothed men on rusty motorbikes bark out their services— *One dollar, I take you now, come friend, now!*—more a command than an offer. The parade of scooters is never-ending, old weary machines with clunky engines terrorizing pedestrians that crowd together for protection to warily cross the streets. The ash, the soot, the grit—it is everywhere, omnipresent, blanketing, suffocating. And everyone, everyone, everyone is plying, hawking, bartering and begging to sell whatever can be pried from this land's miserly hands, their hysterical desperation crying out in pleading vendor eyes as they scratch and claw to generate some veneer of commerce out of the wanton penury of the streets.

These small humble people look at me with eyes that ask, unmistakably: You, brown man, you foreigner, you half-American, among the black-white soldiers with bright teeth and broad shoulders—why are you here? My answer fits only edgewise into the jabbering vignette, somewhere between the screeching child naked on the door stoop and the gray-eyed amputee grandfather sitting folded upon himself like a teetering paper crane, between the neediness and the withoutness and the bellowing hunger of this heavy tactile poverty; my answer fits only edgewise in the accusing quiet of night, when self-secrets are whispered, revelations leaked to an honest silence only to be hastily recanted in the coarse morning light; my answer fits only edgewise when I am courageous enough to state the obvious truth.

I am a conscript for a land far away from my home. I am a mercenary, different from the fortunate sons that brandish deferments like formal pardons. I ceded control of my life a long time ago, when a stray bullet ended one story and started another, when a bitter man struck back the only way he knew how, and when two little boys with sunburned faces and a surfeit of innocence were caught up in a tempest they had no hope of controlling.

I awake again and again and see the same plaintive pleading faces. I awake again and again and the reality is the same, bigger than me, stronger than me, and I must accept it and survive as the Vietnamese do. These people, the Vietnamese, will not leave these mountains or valleys. They were here before the Chinese, before the Khmer, before the French, before us. They will die here. This is their reality. This is Our Reality.

Está norteando, I realize.

Está norteando.

———————●———————

The first official incursion into Cambodia had lasted two months. On the heels of Operation Menu, a massive bombing campaign in eastern Cambodia, US forces led by 1st Air Cav Brigades spent May and June of '70 tracking North Vietnamese, VC and Khmer Rouge soldiers westward through the seasonal monsoon, up and down the hidden tributaries of the Ho Chi Minh trail. According to the Armed Forces Vietnam Network, the American radio station, the mission was a resounding success. They reported that military and civilian casualties were limited and large amounts of munitions were recovered, and that the operation permanently disrupted VC supply routes to II and III Corps.

The real story went slightly different, though. Old-timers in the 7th Cav openly admitted they hadn't found shit in Cambodia. Sure, they came across a decent sized cache of weapons, but China and the Soviet Union would just funnel more in through North Vietnam and Laos. What they hadn't found was Charlie. That's why the secret raids continued into '71.

In a way, it was an honor to be among the few chosen to join the Cambodia missions. The only soldiers selected were Green Berets, Army Rangers and a select number of Airbornes. On the other hand, in a land of praying for lesser evils, it was the worst possible assignment. Because we were conducting clandestine raids in a country where any US military presence would have sent the anti-war American public (not to mention the Cambodians) into mass hysteria, we became *personae non gratae*. A band of well-armed private citizens without papers or uniforms patrolling the jungles and riverbeds of Cambodia *just because we fucking felt like it*. Our generals said they couldn't permit munitions shipments to pass uncontested right under our noses just because the enemy was on the other side of the border. Who were we to argue?

Our Squadron had been conducting the Cambodian raids under Sergeant Lombardi since September. The Cambodia we knew was a foreboding place, densely vegetated and intimate with murder. Each mission began with the knowledge that we might have to fight our way back to Vietnam. While we had managed to return safely each time, Lombardi's oft-repeated mantra circled around our heads before every mission. *Keep expecting the worse, because eventually it's going to happen.* Advice from a man who had survived six straight years of combat carried a lot of weight.

Before departing on missions we were stripped of dog tags, given generic camouflage fatigues and instructed that as of that moment we were civilians—until we made it back. As if we had forgotten. If we were captured, there would be no recon missions. If captured, we would face torturous interrogations. The orders were delivered unequivocally: under no circumstances could we reveal information, no matter what kind of hell they put us through. Simply put, capture was not an option. While the word suicide was never uttered, it was painfully clear that in the face of certain capture, a grenade held tightly to the chest was a viable option.

It was Christmas Eve, 1971 when Lombardi relayed the order that the Squadron would be airlifted to a landing area in eastern Cambodia near the Mekong River. The mission was to intercept and destroy a floating barge carrying anti-aircraft munitions. As always, we donned civilian gear and emptied our personal belongings into rucksacks that Lombardi turned over to his CO. Our prize for returning alive was getting our identities back.

The Hueys left from a grassy airfield outside of Loc Ninh mere miles away from the Cambodian border. They would carry us a few miles over the border, but no further—the closer we got to the Mekong and the capillaries of the Ho Chi Minh trail, the greater the risk that a helicopter would go down. Pilots assigned to the Cambodia missions were under strict orders to avoid aerial combat, even in support of ground troops. And while most recon and search-and-destroy missions used Frogs, Hueys outfitted with rocket launchers, we rode in Slicks, which had only protective armament systems. In every conceivable way, we were on our own.

Shortly after crossing the border the birds touched down and dropped us off. From there we hoofed it through the Cambodian bush, moving northwest to the target point on the Mekong. After three hours of wrestling with the jungle we arrived at the banks of the sweltry river that snaked from Laos to the South China Sea. Phoenix had relayed intelligence about a barge that would arrive in the provincial capital of Kampong Cham that night, which placed its passage through that stretch of river in the late afternoon. The shipment was disguised as a farmer's barge transporting rice sacks, we were told, so we expected minimum resistance.

Lombardi was crouched in a grove of tamarind trees at the cusp of the river bend, nearly invisible through the branches. The rest of the unit was downriver hiding in thick vegetation, slowly sinking into the muddy riverbank as they waited for Lombardi's signal. The afternoon sun beat down boastfully. Sweat pooled in my eyes and rolled down the inside of my fatigues. A congress of gibbon monkeys cavorted overhead in the mango trees, their playful shrieks piercing the slothful afternoon languor.

Upriver, a floating barge emerged from a grove of overhanging branches and began to round the bend. As it turned, the width of the vessel came into view, spanning half of the river. On each side of the barge was a small bamboo hut. In between the two huts were straw chests, wooden crates and rows of rice sacks. Two men in jungle hats and farmer's garb sat on the front of the barge, dangling their feet in the water and maneuvering the raft with long wooden poles.

Lombardi extended his arm. The Platoon opened fire.

The two men sitting in front capsized into the river, their hats floating off with the current. A 66mm rocket struck the center of the barge, igniting an explosion that blew the boat into two parts. The rice sacks were the epicenter of the thunderous explosion, confirming the presence of heavy munitions. As the two remnants of the barge floated to opposite sides of the river, a grenade landed on the flotsam drifting to the far side and razed what remained of the bamboo hut. The force of the explosion launched the mangled bodies of a few enemy soldiers into the river. The barge on the near side remained largely intact, though, and soldiers emerging from the hut began to return fire as they neared the riverbed. All the while, the farmers' wide-brimmed jungle hats floated down the middle of the river, spinning like teacups.

Lombardi ran down the riverbank barking orders to the men. On his left thigh there was a dark blotch of blood.

"2nd Squadron, stay here and lay down suppressing fire. Pollard, Piñera and Piñera, come with me."

We followed Lombardi and rounded the river bend where the barge had landed. The crackle of M-16s droned on behind us, but Charlie was answering with the distinctive thwack of AK-47 fire. A flash of black crossed a stream upriver, barely visible through the foliage. Lombardi dropped to one knee and fired a burst of semi-automatic fire. The gaunt black shadow retreated farther into the tropical rain forest.

The bullet struck Lombardi in the temple as he turned left to track the fleeing soldier. Our fearless Commie leader, an honorable man who had survived Vietnam since '65, collapsed to the marshy ground and died instantly. JC checked for a pulse, gently closed Lombardi's eyes and then rolled the body behind a log. There were no dog tags to remove.

More shots whizzed by from the riverbank but it was impossible to locate their position. JC and I hovered behind a tree stump and fired blindly at the river, pinned down in deep shit.

"Give me cover, I'm going around the left flank." Before we could stop him, Cody was moving through the jungle thicket, headed straight for a wall of Charlie.

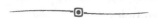

After breaking through Charlie's dug-in position behind a rock wall, Cody rooted out and killed four enemy soldiers. When I saw their position I knew they would have killed us if Cody hadn't charged. It wasn't only his courage that stood out—I had seen swinging dicks that did stupid things looking to prove their bravery. It was that he risked his life for us.

But even then, I couldn't help but worry about him. I worried that the lack of self-preservation would catch up to him. The world is a ruthless taker, and even for the most selfless, the well can run dry.

The Vietnamese were hardwired to expect the worse. Dating back to the early years of French colonial rule, they had built a society capable of accepting violence as the status quo. There were children who had grown up, married and started families without ever having known a day of peace. It amazed me how many Vietnamese, both in the central regions near the DMZ and in the southern Mekong Delta, appeared unaffected by the war. Maybe they believed that this was how the world worked, and how it would always be.

Enduring a twenty-year war replete with a million ARVN soldiers, half a million American GIs, and constant bombings and village patrols was no small feat. VC ambushes and reprisals against alleged South Vietnamese sympathizers added another dimension to the peril, and a notoriously indiscriminate one at that. Yet the Vietnamese took the occupation in stride, unfazed by one more motley crew of soldiers marching through their land. Theirs was a simple, disciplined existence: they labored, shared a modest meal with family and then returned to work amid the constant backdrop of war.

After spending months in country, I still didn't understand the master plan. I knew full well that the stated objective was to fight the North Vietnamese in Indochina to contain the spread of Communism. Understood. Arguable, but understood. Yet I couldn't comprehend our presence from a tactical standpoint. The nature of our engagement in Vietnam—supporting a puppet regime rejected by a majority of Vietnamese voters in past elections—meant that every day we stayed, our presence further demeaned the popular will of the Vietnamese people. Which tends to create enemies. It's also exceedingly difficult to win hearts and minds when your planes are carpet-bombing villages and farms with a flaming petroleum-based jelly that adheres to and incinerates the skin, something not typically seen as an overture of solidarity.

In addition to Napalm there were the 15,000 lb. seismic bombs that obliterated everything and everyone within 300 feet, leaving behind radii of charred nothingness. And that's when I saw a domino effect, after a village was bombed. Lo and behold, the next time we surveilled the area we were inevitably met by sniper fire or fresh land mines. The emergence of new VC activity followed the bombings with an eerie predictability.

And tactically, that's where the logic fell apart. For every soldier we killed or maimed, at least one non-combatant suffered the same fate. Which in turn converted one or more previously non-violent Vietnamese farmers into soldiers avenging the murder of a family member. There was no way to balance the equation, no way to make the morbid math work, no matter how many times you traded bodies back and forth. That's why it felt like we were fighting an entire country.

Soldiers in the 1st Cav were first and foremost trained as airborne paratroopers. Drops weren't as common in Vietnam as they were in WWII or Korea, but they were still used for long distance missions or when helicopters weren't available. Luckily for us, all missions were put on hold after Lombardi was killed until a new CO could be assigned to the 7th. Losing Lombardi was tough on all the men, but our Sergeant would have been happy we got a break from Cambodia. Even if it was his own death that earned it.

The new CO arrived a week later. Lieutenant Harvey Daniels was a blustery man with a foolish mustache, a weak chin and a chest puffed out like a grade school bully. No sooner had he arrived than he was issuing orders for an afternoon parachute jump in the Iron Triangle. Any jump in that enemy-friendly territory was dangerous because Charlie was liable to take pot shots at the conspicuous parachutes, but it was even riskier in daylight. Daniels was not off to a good start.

Cody finished packing his parachute and lit a cigarette. "JC, what's the deal with this mission? I haven't heard shit about the jump zone."

"Headed just north of Phu Cong," JC said as he hustled to finish his parachute. "We'll drop at an open field east of the city and then surveil nearby hamlets."

"What's VC activity like around there?" Cody asked.

"Daniels said an ARVN Battalion moved through just a few days ago and there were no Charlie to be seen."

"And you trust ARVN's intelligence?"

JC finished packing his parachute and looked up. "No, and I don't trust Daniels either. But at least we get to jump."

Cody walked over and slapped JC on the back. "Damn right. Let's get in and out. CYA."

That was only piece of advice that really mattered in 'Nam. Cover Your Ass.

Engagement protocol for the village recon missions was pretty basic. We went house to house searching for signs of VC. If we saw something suspicious we grabbed an ARVN translator to talk to the family, and anyone who fled was considered suspect and would be pursued. The rule was to not shoot unless we knew it was Charlie, or until somebody shot at us. Most soldiers did their best to follow the rules of engagement, despite the ambiguity. Most, but not all.

As long as we landed safely on the jump I didn't expect any surprises from the mission. This type of intelligence gathering was generally harmless (if not also worthless) and any VC in the area usually hightailed it into the bush before we arrived. The good news was that if we encountered resistance we usually had them outnumbered. On a typical mission the biggest danger was sporadic long-distance fire from a few fleeing Charlie. Daniels' decision to jump in the middle of the afternoon didn't do anything to improve our odds, but there were worse things we could have been doing. Although the Iron Triangle was dangerous, it was nowhere near as bad as the Cambodian Mekong. What we did have to watch out for was landing in a village quartering a VC Regiment. We were moving in Squadrons, and there was always a chance that we would stumble upon an enemy army and all hell would break loose.

The C-130 took a flight path south of the Iron Triangle and then pivoted north at Phu Cong. When the plane door opened we stood up and clipped the carabiners onto the wire tag line that ran down the center of the plane. When my jump came I gripped the steel frames of the door and hurled myself out, unleashing a primal scream that startled the bombardier.

As the frigid air whipped against my face, I watched the Squadron soar through the air below me. The first jumpers were landing and the ground looked clear and calm. When the altimeter on my wrist hit 3,000 feet I pulled the rip cord and steered the chute to an open landing spot. The other soldiers were packing their splayed chutes when I hit the ground. I listened for enemy fire but all was quiet.

After landing we moved north toward a trail of smoke rising from a village. Walking on grids of raised earthen paths, we traversed between boggy rice paddies to reach the village. In the fields we passed small groups of Vietnamese women and children. *Xin chào,* we said. They looked up to acknowledge our presence, bowing their heads ever so slightly, and then lowered their eyes back to the work at hand. As we neared the village we could hear shouting to alert the villagers of our arrival. Women and children were extinguishing fires and running to their hootches, knowing that we would order them to their homes to inspect the village.

We split into fire teams and our unit moved to the southern edge of the village. I followed JC and O'Hare as we approached the first hootch.

JC pushed open the bamboo door but it was empty. We searched the next three hootches but they too were empty. Something in the lazy afternoon scene felt wrong.

In the distance we heard shouts from the fire team on the north end of the village. Cody had gone with them and I could hear his booming voice calling for his men to take cover. After he yelled, a burst of gunfire came from the bush.

Rifles raised, we edged around the wall to get a line of sight on the rest of our Squadron. I kneeled down and scanned our southern flank.

A bullet whizzed past JC's shoulder and embedded in a bamboo beam next to us, splintering the thick post in half. We all hit the deck and army crawled to cover.

"I think I saw where the shot came from," O'Hare said. "It was at the end of this row, the far southwest edge of the village."

"You two lay down cover," I said. "I'm headed that way. Follow me."

As soon as JC and O'Hare opened fire I ran. When I reached the last hootch I laid down a burst of cover fire and motioned for them to follow. Through a silence punctuated by occasional rifle cracks, we heard muted rustling sounds in the small bamboo hootch. I pulled out a grenade.

"I'm going to frag it. I move on three. Cover me."

"Wait!" JC implored. "I'm not sure the shot came from there. Let's at least have a look."

"If you're wrong we're dead."

"Just have a look. Please."

"All right. I'll move in first. O'Hare, you take the door. If I fire, you two rock'n'roll."

I duck-walked to the next hootch with JC on my flank. As O'Hare kicked down the door I curled my finger around the rifle trigger.

What I saw then would stay with me forever:

Four small children huddled in the corner, the tops of ghostly white faces peeking above a dirty blanket revealing mops of tousled hair and frightened brown eyes as wide as saucers. Grainy black and white photographs of a young mother and father resting on the only piece of furniture in the room, a scuffed coffee table with chipped corners, the shrine adorned with flowers and a bouquet of burning incense.

As I walked out, eyes cast downward in silent apology, one of the little girls began to whimper and her siblings tried to console her. The words were unintelligible to me, but the feeling was familiar. I knew that terrifying wave of lonely child fear, of siblings confronting an unspeakable reality and trying to convince each other that everything is going to be all right, because there is no one else to say it.

The secret raids in Cambodia continued through the Vietnamese New Year and our Squadron destroyed multiple shipments of arms and munitions. But nothing came without a cost. We lost good men in Cambodia, men who died nameless and alone. Johnson. White. Whitaker. And Lombardi. Men never to be claimed. The men who died were mourned, in the peculiar matter-of-fact military fashion. Especially Lombardi, because he never lied, even when lying would have been easier. But we accepted it, because in war there is no getting around it. It's what war is made for.

Those men stayed with us, walking flank and whispering words of caution as we patrolled the remorseless hollows of that land. They stayed with us then, and after, and always.

You may tell yourself that a person is gone from the world. And you may even fool yourself into believing it's true. But the words of the departed are no more gone than our memories of those who pass. And their truth is no less true, even after their breath can no longer voice it. You can't take the living away, no matter how death comes. You just can't.

Vietnam was a fight for hills, unnamed rocky summits assigned numbers by the Army Corps of Engineers so we knew what the hell we were fighting for. The hills provided the controlling army with artillery coverage over the valleys below. Control the summits, and you controlled the movement of soldiers, tanks and supplies. We fought tooth and nail for mountaintops no bigger than backyards. More than once we lost men taking a hill, only to cede it hours later without firing a shot. No one said any of it made sense.

The North Vietnamese's '72 Easter Offensive caught no one by surprise save the Army brass. They claimed there were no warning signs of the attack, a distortion that went beyond the usual bullshit and into the realm of pure fantasy. The North Vietnamese Army's initial gains proved that Vietnamization was a failure, because the South Vietnamese still couldn't fight without Uncle Sam's bombs, and it showed that the smattering of American troops left in country were fighting an enemy willing to sacrifice a hundred thousand men for twenty miles of scorched hillside. More troublesome was that the NVA seized territory during the initial phase of the Easter Offensive, which didn't go over well with the folks back home. To the American public, fighting a pointless war was bad enough; losing a pointless war was a bridge too far.

Yet the NVA's gains came at a steep price. They were finally fighting out in the open, and all those millions of tons of bombs were finally hitting someone other than peasant farmers. A lot of American and ARVN soldiers died at Hamburger Hill and Dong Ha, but the NVA lost even more. At least we could finally be sure that we were killing the enemy. Nonetheless, the North Vietnamese captured hills, gained ground and established a new perimeter south of the Ben Hai River, Vietnam's Rubicon.

That the initial blow came in the North did not insulate us from the offensive—Charlie was also moving hard and fast in central Vietnam. After crossing the Cambodian border, a full NVA Division attacked Loc Ninh, the lonely outpost we had called home for the past year. Fighting alongside Army Rangers and a South Vietnamese regiment, we held off the advance for two days despite heavy bombardment. ARVN fought bravely, but many South Vietnamese soldiers were taken prisoner when Charlie captured the outpost. JC, Cody and I barely got out in time. We were airlifted to An Loc, the last line of defense between Charlie and Saigon, only minutes before the base was overrun.

Charlie continued their march eastward and reached An Loc within days, and quickly overtook the nearby airfield, squeezing our perimeter to less than a square mile. They later took control of the northern section of town and we were left defending a few city blocks against enemy soldiers dug in across the street. We kept our heads down and made sure there were anti-tank weapons at the ready in case an NVA tank crept around a corner. An Loc was the worst I'd ever seen. I just tried not to die.

The assault slowly morphed into a siege that would last for weeks. Once Charlie had encircled An Loc, the only way food and munitions could be supplied was through airlifts. And so it was: parachuted crates from American planes sustained an entire American Battalion while enemy artillery barraged our shallow bunkers. Everything, deadly and otherwise, rained down from above. There wasn't a single street or muddy backwater path in An Loc that was spared the bombardment. Our saving grace—our only grace—was the Air Force's supremacy. Every time Charlie assembled to launch an offensive, B-52 bombers swooped in with airstrikes to scatter the enemy, granting us another day's pardon until help could arrive.

NVA forces eventually began to peel off and head south, and by late May we had regained control of An Loc and the surrounding territory. Two Army Ranger reinforcement battalions, Charlie's tactical mistakes and a suicidal stubbornness had saved the town. If it had been lost, Charlie would have had a direct route to Saigon. If they had stormed the town, we all would have died in that roadside trench. But the war gods smiled their callous smiles upon us, and we limped on.

After An Loc, elements of the 7th Cav were sent north to Lang Vay Special Forces Camp on the Tchepone River, near the Laotian border. By the time we arrived at Lang Vay it had been nearly two months since the Easter Offensive began, and Charlie had just taken control of Quang Tri city, a stepping stone to the ancient Vietnamese capital of Hue. Hue's importance couldn't be overstated, symbolically or tactically, and we knew the NVA would push farther into South Vietnam with every last man. Their initial thrust had been slowed, but Charlie remained within striking distance of the city. They were either going to be pushed back or break through and take Hue. The line had to hold.

In addition to transporting soldiers and artillery to the new battle lines, Charlie would also have to resupply the offensive. As they moved, the 7th would be stalking their supply routes every step of the way. Sure, we would be even deeper in the belly of the beast, but it was a relief of sorts. At least now we could keep our dog tags during missions.

A decade of bombing had left Quang Tri Province looking like an angry deity had scalped the earth with a jagged razor. The pockmarked mountains and barren valleys provided little cover. The only shelter that did remain was from crippled scarecrow trees long ago charred by a rainbow of carcinogenic chemicals dropped from above, concoctions with playful names like Agent Orange, Agent Pink and Agent Green. The various dioxin- and arsenic-based compounds destroyed life and limb, turning the land sterile—a modern day variant of sowing salt on the fields.

JC and I sat outside the bunker smoking acrid unfiltered cigarettes and eyeing the valley below. Neither of us had smoked before the war or even particularly liked it, but it staved off the boredom and kept us awake at night. And Charlie was without a doubt running supply convoys at night. Despite the lack of cover, stick-figure men lugged 100-lb. packs for miles as they traversed the cratered valleys.

Cody was nervous that night, his eyes roaming over the mountain. He sat hunched on a wooden footstool and cleaned his rifle.

"Be ready, boys," he said. "I've got a feeling we're heading out."

"I feel it too," I said. "They'll be passing through."

"Who's the CO with us tonight?" Cody asked.

"Daniels."

"Fuck. Once more into the breach…." We returned to our smokes.

JC remained quiet. He rocked back and forth, leaning against the turquoise sand bags that lined the bunker walls and the corrugated tin roof. A well-calibrated mortar would decimate this shallow hole steeped in stale rainwater.

The mortars began at 3 a.m. We crouched in the truncated doorway of the bunker, watching the golden-red explosions in the nearby canyons, and awaited orders from Daniels.

The radio crackle interrupted the jittery silence. Daniels' voice was tinny and distant.

"1st Platoon, Rendezvous at Hill 881's southeast bunker at zero four-hundred hours."

The scraggy path down the hill was muddy and treacherous. A misstep meant a free fall down the mountain, because the emaciated tree branches snapped like kindling if grabbed for support. After an hour hike we reached the bunker and signaled our arrival to the 2nd Squadron. Inside the bunker, Daniels was perched on one knee like a football coach. As he talked he peered imperiously over the heads of his men, addressing his sermon to an invisible flock.

"We'll have nearly a full Platoon for this mission. 3rd Squadron will rendezvous with us at the southern base of Hill 861. We're going to need them, too. Phoenix says it's a big supply convoy. Lots of Charlie."

"Sir, what are the coordinates of the rendezvous with 3rd Squadron?" Cody asked.

"I didn't have time to check. We need to move soon. Don't worry, you'll find them down there."

"Sir, Hill 861 is huge."

"Shut up, Pollard. Just find them."

Daniels resumed his speech. "Right. Good. OK. So you'll meet up with the 3rd and move around the east side of the hill. Maintain noise and light discipline. The convoy crossed the Ben Hai an hour ago, so they should be arriving soon."

Daniels stood and dusted off his hands. "Right. Good. OK. So, move out. See you boys back here at zero seven-hundred hours."

Cody laughed out loud. "You mean you're not coming with us?"

Daniels' eyes bulged to cartoonish proportions, the fury scarcely hiding his bruised ego. "Goddamnit, Pollard, you do the soldiering and I'll do the commanding. OK? Now move out!"

Sent into the bowels of enemy territory, our CO staying behind. Right. Good. OK.

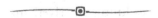

We waited half an hour at the base of Hill 861 and sent scouts to find the 3rd, but without exact coordinates we were more likely to stumble across Charlie than find our own guys. Daniels was a careless and stupid CO, a shake-and-bake officer who abused his power and belittled the men. I hated the man for endangering our lives more than they already were.

After an hour of waiting the night's patience wore thin. We departed the rendezvous point to track the supply convoy alone. To the west, the

Dakrong River crept by and glistened menacingly. The sky was embossed by a million stars, and accompanied by the fulsome buzz of insects. A frog croaked, and the wind moaned.

Ahead, Cody stopped and slowly lowered his arm to the side, signaling for the unit to take cover.

A single rifle crack pierced the air.

O'Hare grabbed his shoulder and dropped to the ground.

"Man down! Take cover!" JC screamed.

Charlie was close but we had no idea where. JC slung O'Hare over his shoulder and carried him to a dugout behind a fallen palm tree. He bandaged the gunshot and covered the wound with a compress. Cody called Freeman over and used the backpack radio to call in a dust-off, but the Medevac said it would be twenty minutes before they could arrive. Seconds later a hail of gunfire exploded from all directions. There were Charlie downriver, and several more were firing from inland. There even seemed to be contact coming from the river itself.

Cody grouped the Platoon together behind the palm tree. "Freeman and Esposito, find and take out the inland VC. We're pinned down so we'll have to fight our way out. Benjamin, you and JC stay with O'Hare, and figure out where the fire is coming from. I'm moving downriver."

Before we had a chance to stop him, he disappeared. We hunkered down and waited for the Medevac.

The pitched cry of a VC soldier rang out downriver. A moment later we heard Cody yell, a guttural groan that echoed across the river. Both JC and I began to run for him.

"Wait," I said. "One of us has to stay with O'Hare. I'll go for Cody."

There was still sporadic fire coming from across the river so I ran to the inside of the palm trees lining the riverbank. Just thirty feet away I saw Cody. His chest was above ground but the rest of his body was hidden from sight, interred in a pit trap. Despite his violent writhing he remained stuck in the ground, probably caught on a punji stake.

"Cody, are you OK?"

"Don't come any closer," he warned. "Charlie's everywhere..."

A blinding, seething pain, a thousand tiny arrows clawing into my shoulder. A warm wetness spreading from my shoulder to my back, my chest and my stomach.

Dizziness, a falling away. A fear, deeper and darker than any I've ever known, that my last seconds were passing, and why was my life not flashing before my eyes, needing to think of something, something, to leave with something.

A rainy spring day. My brother, running with arms wide. A white dress. My mom, watching over us.

Then, darkness.

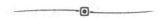

The cell was a made of thick bamboo shoots spaced a few inches apart, and the world was visible only through the narrow slits. Cody was about ten feet away, crouching in a shallow film of water that blanketed the marsh below us. A wooden platform overhead filtered out most of the day's sunlight. In the background I heard men arguing in Vietnamese, clucking at each other in vociferous tones.

"Benjamin, are you okay?"

"My shoulder's FUBAR. You?"

As I spoke footsteps raced down the wooden gangway and a dark silhouette materialized above me.

"No talk!" the guard screamed maniacally, and began to beat me with the butt of his rifle. I covered my head but the blows struck my neck and the festering wound in my shoulder.

The guards stood nearby all day, listening for the slightest noise, and later in the day they again beat us for talking. The one who seemed to most relish delivering the beatings stood closest and flaunted a shiny .38 Hong Kong revolver, menacingly flipping it back and forth between his hands. From the far side of the compound we could hear the muffled sounds of Vietnamese prisoners, but no one dared speak to us. Receiving a beating for talking didn't require much provocation, so Cody and I settled for occasional eye contact, waiting in silence for interrogations we knew would come and clinging to the dwindling hope that our Squadron knew where we'd been taken. As the day stretched into evening, the stench of human waste from the water underfoot became unbearable and I vomited several times.

During a night of sleeplessness and swarming insects, I heard a faint scratching sound coming from Cody's direction. The night was black and I couldn't see what he was doing, but I wasn't surprised he would try to escape. Even if they killed him for it.

By the time the sun peeked over the tree line I was woozy from fatigue and expecting to lose consciousness from the pain of the pus-filled wound. The humidity of the jungle closed in like a constricting anaconda, heavy and relentless. The guards came and took Cody away around midday. They issued him a quick beating before hauling him out of the cage by his neck. Their footsteps receded to a far corner of the compound.

Then, only sounds: the sickly thuds of fists and boots colliding with human flesh; the percussive cracks of whiplashes; creaking noises, like cranking pulleys; low droning groans; and then, the expanses of silence. But he never cried out or begged for mercy. I wondered if I would be as strong.

Hours later they dragged him back to his cage, the heels of his boots catching and clicking on the wooden planks of the walkway, and unceremoniously dropped him back into the cage. He crouched inside with his eyes closed, head down and unmoving, neither seeing nor hearing. I didn't know if he was still alive.

That night I awoke to Cody rattling his cage and shrieking deliriously. The sound of pounding boots closed in on the gangway. I thought he had gone insane until he abruptly stopped screaming.

"When they come to beat me I'm going to escape," he shouted to me. "I'll try to get you out now. But if I can't, I'll come back for you. I promise."

The guard stood astride Cody's cage and jammed his rifle butt through the bamboo cracks. When the guard thrust the rifle in, Cody seized the smooth handle and held on. With the other hand he pulled a large rock from the water below and smashed the lock. As the guard struggled to reclaim his weapon, Cody flipped open the door of the bamboo cage and yanked him inside. The guard slipped and fell on his back, his face barely visible above the muddy water. Cody picked up the rock and slammed it against the guard's temple until the man's brain was protruding from his skull. At the far end of the gangway a volley of footsteps erupted, and a rifle fired in our direction. Cody propelled himself out of the cage.

"I'll come back for you, I promise," he yelled as he ran down the gangway. A bullet whizzed by his shoulder and struck a nearby tree, sending wood shards flying. He jumped off the gangway and disappeared into the black swamp. The guards chased him and sprayed fire in his direction.

A few hours later they returned without Cody. From the look on their faces I could tell he had escaped. After Cody left, the only thing I was sure of was that I was worth more alive than dead because I was the only American prisoner left. I wondered if Cody would come back for me, and I wondered if I would come back if I had been tortured first. I was unsure if loyalty reached those depths.

My turn came the next day. There were questions that I would not, and could not, answer. The punishment came after. First were the beatings and the whippings. They would come to seem pedestrian after what came next, when they tied my elbows together behind my back and fixed the rope to a ceiling beam. I was left hanging with my body folded backward while they beat me. An hour later, or maybe two or three, my arms and torso went numb. The pinched nerves along my spine screamed with pain until they too went numb. The pain made me forget my shoulder; the pain became time and space, the past and the future. Several times I passed out, but they woke me by splashing water on my face, waiting until I regained consciousness to resume. They were very patient.

I didn't sleep that night. Every part of my body was too big for its original space and on the verge of rupturing. My skin could no longer contain my muscles, my bones or my organs. In the fog of pain, I prayed to God and wondered where he was. And I wondered where Cody was, if he had made it back to Lang Vay. I tried to imagine him assembling a rescue team, although in NVA territory that would basically amount to suicide. I wouldn't have blamed him if he didn't come back—there was little chance of saving me. They were slowly but surely breaking my body and my will. I said my last rites, praying for forgiveness for my sins, and waited for the end.

The gunshot jolted me awake. The first thing I saw was the shiny .38 in Cody's hand. He ripped off the shattered lock, threw open the bamboo door and hoisted me onto his back. As he carried me down the platform I saw two NVA soldiers on the ground, blood seeping from assorted knife wounds.

Cody had lurked outside the camp for two days waiting to come back for me. When the NVA sent out search patrols he took cover in a deserted bunker. Only after taking shelter there during the day did he realize that the bunker had been used as a mass grave—the recesses of the cave were filled with human remains.

Despite the pain they had inflicted on his body, Cody carried me on his back through the night until we reached an ARVN fire base near the Dakrong Bridge. Then he carried me up a mountain to find a medic to treat my shoulder. I never understood where that reservoir of strength came from, the strength to block out the pain and the exhaustion and to overcome the same torture that broke my will. I just know he saved me.

The official troop drawdown began in '70, but by '72 it seemed like the only Americans left in Vietnam were CIA, Special Ops and the 1st Air Cav. After Charlie was pushed back to Quang Tri Province and the 17th parallel held as the northern front, we allowed ourselves the slightest hope that we might be sent home soon. And Lord knows we needed to get Cody out of Vietnam.

Following our special treatment at the hands of the North Vietnamese, the Brigadier General gave us two weeks leave in Saigon to lick our wounds and recover. The CO at the base allowed us free rein to roam the city. He probably thought that we would just drink away the bad memories. How much trouble could a couple roughed-up soldiers get into, anyway?

"Two weeks," I said foolishly. "It's like a summer camp. What's two weeks going to do?"

Two weeks was plenty. Cody shot up for the first time during that leave in Saigon. I can't say for sure why he started using smack. I don't know that it was the torture, necessarily, although that must have played a part. My best guess is that his dream of being the good American soldier had been gutted by the reality of that godforsaken war. For a kid who had grown up with Army posters on his wall, the disillusionment must have been unbearable. But who knows, really. Who ever knows.

Cody became an addict remarkably fast. He was an easy mark, even more than most first-time users. It wasn't just his body that craved the fix; he quickly came to believe that his mind needed it. Knowing little about the valence of drug addiction, I expected it to be a drawn-out process, a controlled regression. But heroin instantly became the most important thing in Cody's life, and everything else withered away. The addiction was insatiable, and getting him ready for combat missions became a herculean task. And despite the stalemate and the percolating rumors of peace talks, the missions continued.

I didn't blame him for using heroin, at least not in the beginning. In him I saw a naïve man-child, pure of heart. I saw his shame at the metastasizing hate seeping through him, and regret at the stupidity of his former innocence. I saw the slow but certain coming apart of my best friend.

As for me, I drifted back to a day when drops of honey rain fell from incandescent skies and a mother in a white dress watched over her sunburned and freckle-faced boys. The sad beauty of that celestial day kept me whole and made the present less real. It carved out a space for me to take refuge.

We never bothered asking why American troops were in Vietnam. Our questions would have been ignored, or even punished. But we weren't winning and we weren't losing. We just traded soldiers like chess pawns and then tried to justify the collateral damage afterward. It was a tasteless joke, a grim fable, the astronomical number of people that were killed in Vietnam. Thousands. Hundreds of thousands. *Millions.* Sure, some of them were VC. But we killed less VC than the official numbers reported, and less than we wanted to believe. That stubborn lie spawned a grisly phrase often heard in country: *If it's dead, it's VC.*

Classified information in Saigon didn't stay that way for very long. Officers and soldiers desperate for information about withdrawal plans became a lot less concerned about protocol when their lives were on the line. One evening we came across a short-timer with mere days left on his tour. The surly Major was on a nasty bender drinking his way out of Vietnam, and we took advantage of his inebriation to pry away information. In the midst of his drunken trance he revealed that the 1ˢᵗ Air Cav would be heading home at the end of June.

"June? Of this year? 1972?" I asked.

"Yes, June."

"June?" I asked again dumbly, disbelieving.

"Yes, I said June," he repeated. "Now go away so I can drink in peace. I'm finally getting out of this hellhole."

The Major's information turned out to be correct. On June 24 the Army announced that the 1ˢᵗ Air Cavalry Division would be withdrawn from Vietnam. Chinooks transported the 1ˢᵗ Batallion to Hue on June 26 and to Saigon on June 27. Within days we would be on a plane back home.

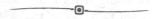

It was never fully explained why our tour was extended. We were specialized soldiers in covert roles, we were told, and the normal rules didn't apply. The Army was not looking for feedback.

Daniels also never explained why he waited until Saigon to reveal our orders. It seemed like the kind of thing that was too important to have slipped his mind. But import, after all, is in the eye of the beholder. We would be sent back to Loc Ninh, the remnants of an emaciated US Army fighting alongside the dangerous ineptitude of the South Vietnamese.

Back to Cambodia, to relinquishing dog tags before missions, to flying over and ducking under a wall of Charlie to attack supply convoys, to anonymous comrades left behind. August passed and we lost Van Atta, a good-hearted kid from rural Ohio, built like a brick shithouse and always ready with a dirty joke to lighten the mood. In September we lost Sanchez, a first-generation Chicano from a dusty Texas border town who had signed up to prove his patriotism. In October and November, we lost O'Hare and Freeman. This time O'Hare took one in the neck and no Medevac was going to save him. Daniels caught one in December, a small piece of poetic justice. But when I heard the news, I felt nothing. It wouldn't bring those men back.

Despite the missions, the lost comrades and our desperate pleas, Cody kept using. He overdosed twice and lost consciousness both times. It wasn't hard to see that heroin was killing him, but the officers that passed through

Loc Ninh couldn't be bothered to raise a finger for some drug-addled grunt. *We need every man we can get,* they were fond of saying.

By the start of 1973, the rumors about a treaty were humming louder than ever. But by that point we didn't know what to believe. On January 20 we were told by our new CO, Lieutenant Pyle, that the interdiction raids would be suspended until further notice. We spent the week waiting, smoking and betting on whether we would make it home by the end of January. JC, ever the cynic, put twenty bucks against it. Going against every fiber of my being, I took the wager.

The Paris Peace Treaty was signed on January 27, 1973. The news proclaiming an end to American involvement in Vietnam was broadcast across South Vietnam. *Peace with honor,* they said. Whatever the hell that meant. But it was over, and we were going home.

I remembered something our mom used to say to Father when he got especially impatient, when things weren't turning out the way he wanted.

No hay mal que dure cien años, she would say, *ni cuerpo que lo resista.*

There is no evil that lasts a hundred years, nor a body that can resist it.

Mom was right, as usual. Our nightmare was finally over, and just in time, because we wouldn't survive any longer.

I now see it was premature to believe that winning the bet was possible. After spending so much time in Vietnam, such optimism was unforgivable.

On January 29, Lieutenant Pyle informed select members of the 7th Cav that instead of going home we would return to Loc Ninh to conduct peacetime missions in Cambodia. Not only would we again be surrendering dog tags, but the interdictions would be even more dangerous because of the Khmer Rouge's growing power. There was also the trifling detail of Loc Ninh being Charlie's first stopover when they inevitably re-crossed the Cambodian border to attack Saigon.

Peacetime observation and monitoring missions, Pyle had said. They all spoke like that, those highfalutin West Point men, reciting vapid euphemisms that were lies before they were ever spoken, and believing themselves clever for having done so. When he phrased it—*thusly*—I realized that it requires a special contempt to spout verbose bullshit and expect it be accepted as truth, chapter and verse. A lie is a lie is a lie, even in its Sunday's best. Even when the preacher tells it.

Upon hearing the news, Cody shot up a vial of heroin. We found him with a whisper of breath, within minutes of death. His lips were an ashen blue and his arms and legs trembled as he choked on his own vomit. I pumped his chest with all my strength, praying that the shell-shocked lungs beneath would breathe. When he finally regained consciousness he rolled into a giant ball on the cold wooden floor, knees pulled tight to his chest, and cast his eyes to the ground. I had never seen someone live after having been so close to death.

Operations, dust-offs, KIAs; requisitions, invoices and supply convoys—the war had ended, but its inertia continued unabated. War was good business for the poppy producers and heroin dealers, too, both American and Vietnamese, and they were in it for the long haul along with us. Even when it was impossible to get new flak jackets or munitions, there was always some smack that could be found. Although they lost paying customers as American forces withdrew, they made sure product was available to all the remaining junkies. Cody kept on using.

Although we discussed the matter for hours on end, the decision was actually quite simple. We needed to get out of Vietnam. More importantly, we needed to get Cody out before he killed himself. If the end of the war was not going to get us home, what would?

We sat up talking into the early morning. Cody was coming down after getting high the night before, and his attempts to stay awake were failing. In his bedraggled state he kept falling asleep and hitting his head against a wooden beam, interrupting the conversation every few minutes with dull thumps.

"How can they keep us here?" I asked.

"They can do whatever they want," JC said.

"Don't they know the war ended?"

"Maybe 'the end' means something different to them?"

Cody toppled over again and cracked his head against the beam. His eyes opened slightly, but he was still too groggy to comprehend anything. I pushed his back against the wall to keep him upright.

"You mean the word?" I asked.

"Yeah, maybe there's a fake end, and then there's the *real* end," JC said.

"But what if the next 'end' is phony, too? What if we're here even longer?"

"How can they keep us here indefinitely? They can't." JC's statement was exceedingly reasonable. In Vietnam, that usually translated to exceedingly wrong.

"Come on," I said. "You haven't heard the stories of specialized soldiers trapped in combat that never make it back home?"

"Guess what," I added. "We're specialized."

"Yeah. I know," he said. "Maybe the end is when we're dead. That would have to be the end, wouldn't it?"

Cody toppled over again, this time only gently bumping his head. He had finally fallen asleep.

"The end will be when they tell us," I said. "For Cody, that won't be soon enough. I'm not going to sit here and watch him OD while our CO acts like he's fine."

"So what do we do?"

"We have to leave. All of us. We can go to Thailand. Then bribe a ship crew to take us to California. I've heard of grunts making it back that way."

"But we'll be deserting the Army."

"They deserted us a long time ago."

"And what about Father?"

We hadn't talked about our father in months. I wondered if he was still alive, but I figured that they would have told us if he had died.

"In the end, he's still our father." I looked JC in the eyes. "He's not the same man, I know. But he has to take us in. We're the only family he has left."

JC was quiet for a while. He looked around the dreary barracks, staring at the rows of empty cots that ran like railroad tracks down each side of the glorified tent. And then he looked at Cody. Our friend's face was gaunt, his skin jaundiced in the wan lantern light. JC knew what I said about Cody was true. Even if he resented the burden, he knew we owed him our lives.

"All right. Let's go."

And so it came to be that we deserted the most powerful military in the world.

On February 1, 1973, three privates from the 1ˢᵗ Air Cavalry Division, 3ʳᵈ Brigade, 7ᵗʰ Cavalry Regiment hopped a midnight Chinook convoy and headed to Saigon. After arriving in the early morning, they hired an old Vietnamese man to smuggle them to the Mekong Delta in the back of his rundown jalopy. Hours later he dropped them off in Xom Ba Tra, a small Vietnamese village on the Gulf of Thailand. That night they stayed in an abandoned shanty near the beach. The next morning they woke at dawn and met a fisherman willing to take them to Thailand, paying the man two weeks' wages to make the dangerous trip.

The three hundred mile boat journey to the Thai border lasted all day. The grunts hid underneath a tangled fishing net that reeked of rotten catfish. The ship captain, a spindly Cambodian, chain smoked cigarettes and nervously eyed the horizon, and the small chugboat somehow managed to evade the US Navy as it crossed the ocean waters. The ship arrived to the port town of Muang Trat in the late evening, just as the sun set in the west over mainland Thailand. The young soldiers paid a truck driver five *bhat* to let them ride in his truck bed to Bangkok.

They arrived to the brewing chaos of Bangkok just before midnight struck. The next day they found a post office and posted a letter.

February 3, 1973

Father:

I don't expect you to understand this. But if ever we've needed you, we need you now.

We are no longer in Vietnam. While I can't go into the circumstances that forced us to leave, I hope that you trust in the judgment of your sons. We had to leave.

We are safe for now, but we can't stay here. The US military is everywhere in Southeast Asia and there's nowhere to hide. Every day that we are here threatens our safety and our freedom.

> *We need your help. There is a way for us to get to California, but we need your help.*
>
> *I pray that you can forgive us. I know that we have disappointed you, but I beg your forgiveness.*
>
>

Your son,
Benjamin
>

Thailand was a blur, a nightmare better left behind but impossible to forget. Waiting...just waiting.

———————◎———————

February 16, 1973

Benjamin:

> *You are right. I am disappointed. You have failed in your duty. You have disgraced yourselves and your family.*
>
> *You cannot come home. If they find you, they will deport all of us. I cannot go back to Chile. The Communists will kill me.*
>
> *We don't always get what we deserve. Sometimes we get more, but often we get less. It's a harsh reckoning, accepting that life isn't fair, but it's a lesson that is best learned early.*
>
>

Your father
>

In the end, I wasn't all that surprised by the letter. Our father had turned his back on us long ago, blinded by a narrowing world of victimization. But his words followed me day and night. *We don't always get what we deserve.* Maybe the words haunted me so because I had come to believe them.

The next day we boarded a freighter leaving Bangkok. We had a vague plan, nothing more, but we needed to get out of Thailand before someone turned us over to the Army. Before we left, I posted one last letter, hoping for a reprieve from the end of the world. One Last Chance.

On the ship, looking through a porthole at an endless sea framed by a pallid crescent moon and the undulating darkness below, I promised myself I would never forget.

All my memories are with the men we left behind, the ones who bled out in rice paddies and dark-hearted jungles and died terrified and alone. Those memories can never fade away. They can never die. I gave more in that country—more blood, more sweat, more tears, more brothers—I gave more in that country than I'll ever give in my own.

PART III

SHELL BEACH, CALIFORNIA: PRESENT DAY

It's another sleepy afternoon on the Central Coast, a slow and breezy Saturday. The cool winds are blowing southward toward LA and its glib SoCal environs, imparting a picture-perfect day on this unassuming stretch of beach. On the coast, winds blowing in from the Northwest are typically cold and moist, and leave behind a heavy inland fog. But even when those chilly winds arrive, the Central Coast is generally spared the ensuing winds and storms. Just one more way in which this place I now call home is different, and sheltered. In Chile, even the slightest intimation of a northern wind meant a storm was on its way.

Looking out the window of the study, the red rocks of the Pacific Coast are glimmering in the midday sun. In the distance, tiny shimmering surfboards are maneuvered by tinier tanned surfers skimming the waves, deftly rising up and then disappearing underneath the breaking curves. In this place, the days go by with an alarming indifference. It's almost like they don't go by at all.

Today is a normal day, in the sense that my shoulder hurt in the morning when I first woke. In the sense that I went for my daily run, survived my daily run-in with the seagulls and took a swim afterwards in the Pacific. In the sense that I will stop by the office later today to check up on my properties, dally a little shuffling papers pretending to be busy, and then return home in the evening to rattle around the house and watch the sunset while nursing a tall tumbler of scotch. I'll quietly kiss Hope as she falls asleep, so as not to wake her, and then wander the house with a mind full of jumbled thoughts from other times. In the sense that this routine has filled my days and nights for so long that I don't remember any other. Or rather, I know that life was different at some point—I know because I have dates and pictures and faces seared in my memory, and a history replete with more stage entrances and exits than I can bear to remember— to prove that it all happened. But these days, I can hardly claim that it was mine. It's been so long that it seems this strange story belongs to an old friend with whom I long ago lost contact.

My attorney is coming by the office in the evening. I've decided that it's time to make a living will. It's not that I feel like I'm close to dying; even though I am a little overweight and probably drink more than is good for me, I'm in relatively good health for a grandfather. Upon reflection, though, it was clear how crazy it was to have waited this long. Of all people, I should have known that no one has ever been granted the unbreakable promise of a tomorrow.

As I get older, I get lost more and more in my thoughts. My memory may be going, but I'm trying hard to preserve some things, to attach details and texture to the formless nostalgia that lays siege with growing frequency, and leaves bittersweet remnants in its wake. When I walk along the beach I see the carefree teenagers and statuesque twenty-somethings playing volleyball and leisurely tanning, and I try to remember when life was like that. It never was, but I try to remember all the same.

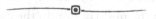

I hear the kids these days are backpacking around Asia. Some even make it as far as Vietnam, I'm told. Who has a year in their life to drop everything and go wandering? My middle son, as it turns out. Nathan recently left on a backpacking trip through Europe and Asia. I suppose sauntering around third world countries and getting high with Aussies and expats is a rite of passage, too, something akin to my generation's misadventure in Vietnam. The kids fighting over in Iraq and Afghanistan probably feel like I used to, a gauzy scattershot resentment of the unaffected masses, the ones getting off scot-free. But what do I know? What I don't know could fill a warehouse.

The parallels are there, if you think about it. We were also dumb kids who went halfway around the globe to trudge through backwater villages, and the few things we did know were also a lot more dangerous than all that we didn't. But the differences are harder to swallow: we had more than half a country trying to kill us, and we were killing a lot of them. But it's a different generation, and I thank God my children can choose their lives, for better or worse. As ungrateful as this generation can be, it's better to be unmoored than embittered.

I can only imagine what Nathan's up to over there. Knowing him, he's probably romancing some sultry European girl as we speak, drinking and dancing in a dive bar somewhere between Hanoi and Kuala Lumpur. He's spent the last few years casting about between jobs and cities and girlfriends, and though he's got a good heart I worry about him—he's too reckless for his own good, desirous of everything all at once. I pray that he chooses the life he wants before a different one chooses him, and that he finds a good woman to anchor that life. The one that lets him willfully put that all behind. I just so happened to have met mine when I was twenty-one years old. I had my life drawn out like an architect's blueprint, and she was the keystone.

My life is a montage of regrets, numbering too many to count. But deserting the Army is not among them. We were left behind, even after the Paris Peace Accords officially ended American military involvement in Vietnam. Even after The End. The raids continued, and men kept dying, and Cody slipped farther down into the vortex of addiction.

Deserting the Army is not among my regrets, but leading us to Chile is. If only Father had forgiven us, we might have been safe. If only.

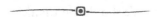

I saw Phuong yesterday when I raced over to the liquor store because I ran out of scotch too early in the evening. When I arrived she was flipping over the *Closed* sign.

"Hello, Mr. Piñera," she said through the glass door.

"Hi, Phuong. I know you're closing, but can I buy a bottle first? It will just be a minute."

She thought for a moment and then unlocked the door. "Of course."

I headed straight for the scotch aisle, a well-worn route of mine, selected a few bottles of my drink of choice and walked up to the register.

"It's a beautiful night," I said.

"Yes, it is. The sky is beautiful," she said.

"How is everything with your family in Vietnam?"

"Everything is well, Mr. Piñera. Thank you for asking."

"My son Nathan is backpacking in Vietnam this summer. He's traveling from Saigon to Hanoi."

"That's great. I'm sure he'll enjoy his trip." She was polite as always, but I could tell she was hesitant to resume our ongoing conversation about her homeland.

"So have you been back to visit your family recently?" I asked.

"My husband and I went back to Saigon last year when my niece had a baby girl. The family just keeps getting bigger."

"Congratulations. It must be exciting to have the whole family together in one place."

"Yes, it is. I miss them very much." With that she handed me my change, a subtle signal that the conversation had run its course. I decided to try one more time.

"And how is the country? Is it safer than it used to be? Are the people happy that it's developing?"

"Oh, Benjamin. You and your questions about Vietnam. When will it end?" Far from mocking or cruel, she was worried about me. She wore the look of a concerned mother.

"When will what end?"

She placed her small hand over mine. "You already fought in the war, and you survived. You can't keep living in the past. We were both lucky to have made it out alive. We should be thankful, and move on with our lives. It's what the people who we lost would have wanted."

With that, I realized how foolish and transparent my entreaties for information had been all along.

"But I can't, Phuong. The things that I did—they stay with me. Maybe I can't forget because I don't deserve to."

"Benjamin, I lost my father and two sisters when the Viet Cong attacked our village. Then my mother and I lost our home and all of our possessions when an American bomb landed on our village. We lost everything. But there is nothing to do but keep going."

She put the bottles in a paper bag and handed them over.

"You have to forgive yourself. You owe that to your family."

I nodded and turned to leave, amazed by this blessed woman, this gentle soothsayer, who has understood these demons better than I ever have.

As I was leaving, she called to me from behind the counter.

"One last thing. Not that I don't appreciate the business, but you have to stop drinking so much. You're turning into a fat American." She laughed and waved me on my way.

I don't know how to find forgiveness in this world, and I don't know how one climbs out of the depths of loss to find redemption. But I would give anything to make things right.

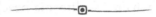

A thing gets remembered for a reason, even if you don't know why. Our mother used to say that. She believed the Lord safeguarded certain things, knowing that we would need them again. The words that Lombardi spoke, I never understood why I might come to need them. But Mom also said the Lord works in mysterious ways.

Lombardi had said it casually, the thing I couldn't forget, an offhand comment as if it were the day's weather forecast. That was when he first told us about the soldiers, VCs and GIs alike, who decapitated enemy corpses out of hatred, or madness, or something in between.

"Hell yes, they're out there," he said. "If you want to see the worst in men, you've come to the right place."

"That isn't true, is it?" I asked. "Do you really believe that?"

"Son, how could I invent something so terrible?"

I didn't want to believe what he said, so I didn't—until I saw it with my own eyes. Then I could never forget. War is meant to kill people, and there's no getting around that, but the how matters too. When such things come to pass, the how has to matter, and it's impossible not to remember.

But I also couldn't help but wonder why I couldn't forget Lombardi's words. Were flashbacks of headless corpses and disembodied heads not vivid enough on their own? But maybe recalling my disbelief at Lombardi's words had a reason, too. Maybe it was to remind me of when I still believed that men weren't capable of such things. We hold onto the things, turning them over and over in our mind until the sheer exhaustion of it is too much to handle.

We left Chile as boys and arrived to California as young men. At seventeen we were nearly adults, or at least we thought ourselves so, and we were both taller than Father, making us tall for Chileans and just about average in California. We also towered above most of the Latinos, which helped minimize the number of times we were mistaken as Chicanos, although it still happened on nearly a daily basis. That, and the relatively fair skin and freckles inherited from our father's side, meant we didn't stand out from the sandy-haired California beach boys as much as the other Latinos. But looking and feeling are two very different things. I felt more foreign in California than any first-generation Mexican immigrant. We had no family—no people—and there was no trace of what our lives used to be.

Brotherly competition and our father's passion for the game had driven us to play soccer at an early age. Since childhood we had played in *pichangas,* pick-up games outside of school or at the beach. We were both talented players, although JC was usually the best player in any game we joined. Sticking to routine, we ran and trained every day on the beach.

Soccer wasn't the only thing that attracted us to the beach, though. All the stunning blond girls, those famous California specimens, also kept us coming back. While passing the ball around, we conjured up possible scenarios to talk to them. Do we accidentally kick the ball their way, or just walk up and say hello? But our planning was all for naught; we were cowed by our language deficiencies, too intimidated to start even the most basic conversation. It is infinitely more difficult to be charming in a foreign language, and we figured we would just scare them away with our thick Chilean brogue.

So we practiced, admired girls from afar and studied English to prepare for classes. And even though we were nearly 6,000 miles away, we learned of our native country's imploding fault lines. The blurbs buried on Page 20 of the LA Times, worlds away from the wrenching Vietnam saga that dominated the front page, told of a country usurped by Marxist dictators. The story recounted therein was a simple one and seemingly unconnected to the protests swelling all over America, or even to the daily departure of hundreds of soldiers to Vietnam. It was as if people didn't understand that Chile, just like Vietnam, was one more pawn on the same chessboard. Even though no definitive effort had as of yet determined its fate, its time would come.

In those first few months, Father was gone most of the time. Even when he was around the blank stare belied his physical presence. He was lost in another time, scarcely interested by the here and now. He didn't read the stories about Chile, or any other newspaper articles for that matter. The outside world had ceased to matter to him in part because he had ceased to matter to it. He had been an important man in Chile, but now he was just one more immigrant in a land chock full of them, and he was embarrassed about his loss of importance. The loss of pride was caused in part by his limited comprehension of our new and guttural language— regressing from an intelligent man to a decidedly simple one over the course of an international flight is a humbling experience. Determined that we wouldn't suffer in the same way, he pushed us to improve our English and erase any trace of an accent. To be less Chilean.

We were scheduled to begin classes in the fall of 1970. After missing the first month of the semester we were already behind. Our English, though improving, was still miles away from genuine fluency. And we didn't know a soul. Thus fully prepared, we were tossed into the byzantine shark waters of the American high school, an iconic world that had come to seem so commonplace through movies. Thank God we at least went in together. I can't imagine braving that shock without JC's steady bulwark of support. Then, as it would be again, it was us against the world.

The school principal placed JC and I in the same classes, believing that the close proximity would help us *successfully acculturate*, in his words. It was good to have JC's support, but it also doubled the spectacle. Instead of one foreigner who appeared in the middle of the semester there were twin brothers. They knew we weren't Mexican, which was clear from the

lukewarm reception we got from the Chicanos. But even after learning that
we were Chilean, no one managed to piece together a possible connection
between our arrival and the election or the attempted coup. No one seemed
to know what was happening in Chile.

The California of then is basically like the California of today, save
the adolescent dot-com billionaires and the fake tits on every woman
over sixteen from here to Tijuana. It's an addictive elixir of materialism,
hedonism, escapism, envy and anything goes capitalism, all cobbled
together by a puzzlingly calm ocean and outrageous property taxes. It is a
place for dreamers and discontents, where the people go who know they
don't want to be wherever they are—a final frontier in a country bereft
of frontiers. I love it, and I hate it. But it has been my home since we left
Chile in 1970, excluding my tour in Vietnam—and of course, our return
to Chile, a small but profoundly deep inkblot on a life's humble chronology
that, despite its brevity, has bled into its adjacencies and permanently
stained them all the same.

To have spent my income-generating years here in arguably the
wealthiest place in the history of civilization was simply a stroke of good
fortune. Despite an aversion to the beloved American daily grind I migrated
toward real estate, first working as a carpenter on a few homes in the early
70's. A few years later I managed to buy a rental property, which benefited
from the real estate boom and provided capital to buy more properties,
including the home my children grew up in and where Hope and I still live.
While considered only middle class here on the California Coast, I am rich
beyond my wildest dreams. Perhaps this is what my father imagined when
he moved us here so many years ago, his light at the end of the tunnel. But
I'll never know for sure.

I am an outsider, a position I have come to appreciate for the vantage
point it affords. The truth is, I'll never be an authentic piece of this
exceptional American machine. I am a survivor, no more. I have seen
death, glimpsed the awful glint in her jet-black eyes, and I have seen the
terror inflicted by the conviction of the righteous. So I tread carefully, even
in my adopted home, even in the land of the free.

It seems that once again I've become lost in the past, something that
happens more and more all the time. My wife and our three children know
these melancholic nor'easters all too well. Years ago my son Nathan, armed

with the brutal honestly of the intoxicated after returning home late from a beach kegger, described me as *a castaway who returned to civilization after a lifetime away, and wouldn't accept that everything had changed.* Like me, he has a flair for the theatrical. Unlike me, he's found a healthy way to utilize it, as a fledgling screenwriter.

Hope loves living near the ocean, close enough to hear the waves at night. She's a transplanted Midwesterner, a bustling little blond with the deep blue eyes of her Scandinavian ancestors. Although the years have worn her simple beauty, they have not stolen it. She missed most of her parents' final years living here, unable to travel much with work and the kids' activities taking center stage, but being by the ocean reminds her why she came in the first place. I have always envied her commitment to the decision.

Quite simply, I've loved her for loving me the way she does, with such stalwart conviction. I arrived in pieces, silenced by loss and embittered by suspicion. Not all that unlike my father, actually. Yet she took me in, breathing new life into me and bringing me back to the land of the living, or as far as I was going to make it. For that alone, it was impossible not to love her.

My children are grown, two good-hearted men and a princess daughter full of grace with a soul capable of moving mountains. Just like her grandmother, my mother. They all live close enough to visit, and my oldest son Thomas and his wife have a baby son. They named him Juan Carlos. I am a grandfather. This is a good life, by any measure.

Yet the world is inexorably different from the one I knew as a child, marked by an unsettling timbre that echoes around my head. A world that could never be mistaken for the previous version. All that's left are the people left behind, and the triviality of my haunted memories. There is no going back and no undoing what's been done.

I've never told Hope about Ayelen, or how so much of me had been carved out and scraped away when we fled Vietnam and returned to Chile. I just can't. It would break her heart to know I had given myself over to another woman before I knew her, and it helps no one to keep that memory alive. Ayelen was erased. Not passed on, nor returned from whence she came. She was taken.

I wish I had been one of those zealous intellectuals from good families who felt empowered to criticize war without ever having lived it. I think of those young men and women, well-meaning and morally assured, and I wonder if they've ever hoped, like I do, that today was not today, and tomorrow was not tomorrow.

As I wade deeper through these remembrances, frayed dog-eared pages from my plebeian history, I fade from the here and now. Hope looks at me and feels like she's losing the only part of me she has left. My regret for doing this to her is as deep and as wide as the ocean. The man she sees, and the man she continues to wait for, is a man of constant becoming, an eternal work in progress. And her patience with this state of atrophy, this failure to materialize and harden, only makes it hurt all the more. But what can I give her when what I would give is no longer in my possession. How do you give what you don't have?

Were it possible, I would leave the past's flotsam in its rightful place. But I am growing old, old enough to ponder a world without me in it, and these disintegrating pages must be read aloud. Rehashed. Reborn. The past replays without remorse, a broken record, an old refrain. JC. Cody. Suyai. Ayelen. Demanding to be heard.

Even forgetting has a breaking point, when it can no longer endure the magnitude of what is being forgotten. Then the memories come crashing down from the shelves and cabinets of our minds where they have been sequestered. And what we're left with is a jumbled chaos that's even more confusing than before, but one that must be repackaged, must be made to make sense again all the same. Four decades is a lifetime of forgetting. As my story nears to a close, I know it has been too long. I can't go on forgetting forever.

PART IV

CHILE: 1973

Valparaiso!

JC, Cody and I arrived on the shores of the 16th century port city in the early days of March, in time to catch the tail end of the glorious Chilean summer before the winds passing over the Andes grew cold. On the mammoth freighter transporting copper between the New World and Asia, we slept in the cargo area below deck, sneaking upstairs to beg, borrow and steal rations from sailors. The crew was comprised primarily of Chileans, faithfully identified by their lilting, staccato accents riddled with *chilenismos* so provincial you could hardly understand the dialect one region to the next. Mixed among them were Argentines, Peruvians, Bolivians and a handful of Vietnamese who had somehow escaped their country's plight through extraordinary ingenuity and pidgin Spanish. As for our passage, we had bribed the ship captain with nearly all of our money, a combination of old piastre bills, Vietnamese dong, and fifty bucks Cody had managed to swindle in a card game. Or so he said. We didn't delve too deeply into the why's and how's with him anymore.

After almost two years in Vietnam I never could have imagined anything more miserable than a rainy season in country with foot rot and water that gravitated upward from the ground. But I had never been as sick in my life as I was on that boat. The stale bread and scraps of cured meat we managed to scrape together served only to remind us of our hunger, and the wound in my shoulder pulsated with pain throughout the trip, an unwanted souvenir courtesy of the VC. Even fleeing from the war and ignominiously AWOL, Vietnam took its pound of flesh.

The voyage lasted three weeks, with calls in China, Hong Kong, South Korea, Japan, Peru and finally Chile. The hold where we spent those sickly days was a dank, dimly lit grotto dominated by spider webs, rats and the caustic grind of steel containers grating against each other and the ship's hull. One morning, after three weeks on the ship, I awoke to JC shaking me with a manic expression on his face.

"We arrive in Valparaiso this afternoon. I overheard the sailors talking yesterday."

"How long will the ship be in port?"

"One night. We're home, finally."

We waited until darkness fell before climbing out of the cargo hold. As we crossed the deck, the mariner winds howled across the bow of the ship like a wailing widow. Rucksacks in hand, we jumped onto the wharf over a dark chute that vanished into the obsidian waters below. Weaving between the storage areas and the rail tracks, we found an unused loading dock and took refuge inside. Sheltered from the wind, we divided up and devoured the last piece of bread and then pushed together sawdust scraps to use as pillows on the cold cement.

We were home, finally, to the land of our birth and childhood. To our *Patria*. Though I remember looking at Cody in the pale yellow moonlight and thinking that he had come to seem alone, even in the presence of others. Once again a stranger in a strange land, without a place to call home.

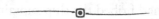

There was a period of time—starting Since I Can Remember and ending on a cold and rainy night in 1964—when I remember our family as being a single unbreakable thing, with a size and a depth and a weight, a deep-down kinship that banded us together and defined our allegiances. There were always going to be disagreements, because our Mom and her sister, Suyai, were too close for the proximity of their lives not to occasionally collide and leave bruised feelings. Father and Cristián, Suyai's boyfriend, had also clashed in the past, two men of very different minds forcefully airing those differences, but for a time they shelved their grudges for the good of the family. During those years, the presence of family was a real thing, a protective cocoon that was safe and indivisible. Permanent. That was a period of time, with a soft beginning and a knife-edged end.

Closer to the end than the beginning, Cristián and Suyai got married, and Suyai was pregnant shortly thereafter. To celebrate the news we all took a trip to the beach in Valparaiso. Traveling in Cristián's truck from Santiago, JC and I sat in the bed and poked our heads above the cab to feel the rushing wind on our faces. The adults crowded inside the cab of the truck. Mom sat on Father's lap and Suyai sat in the middle, her round belly wedged between my mom and Cristián in the driver's seat. Through the windows we could hear them laughing, our mother's voluble giggles rising above and bursting through the wind.

We spent the whole day at the beach building sand castles and diving in the waves. In the afternoon we cooked fresh seafood and ate jumbo slices of juicy watermelon that stained our mouths and our clothes. As the day stretched on languorously and the sun began to set, our parents rested on blankets and drank wine while JC and I played soccer with a group of boys near a lighthouse down the beach.

On the way home, as Mom drifted off to sleep with her head on Father's chest and Suyai leaned against Cristián's shoulder, Suyai said something I've never forgotten.

¿Sabes que? Fue un día perfecto. Un día perfecto.

It was a perfect day, you know? A perfect day.

JC and I held on tight to the truck's rusted frame, occasionally laughing and punching each other but mostly just staring up at the night sky. The stars began to appear, kindly aligning for our imaginations, and we lay on our backs and dreamed up a universe watching over us.

That was a long time ago, before Father and Cristián's last argument became their last argument and they said things that couldn't be taken back, and then said them again. It was before Mother was *forbidden* to do everyday things like go to the market with her sister, and it was before Father's eyes developed a steely coldness that you felt deep down when he looked at you. That was before family became a thing of the past, and the cocoon unraveled before our little-boy eyes, and there wasn't anything we could do about it. I remembered how it used to be, and I hoped Suyai did too.

The cliffs of the city ascended to downtown, beckoning visitors to climb its byzantine streets and stray into the stinking Technicolor frenzy of a port city. Valparaiso was built without rhyme or reason, homes and buildings squeezed into forgotten crevices like tiny pastel-hued baby teeth jutting haphazardly in all directions. Daylight peaked over the Cordillera to the east and cast speckled rays on the yellows, purples, oranges and reds of the painted rooftops. Sailors came home between voyages and recklessly spent their wages on women and booze, injecting the suggestion of latent violence. In crooked alleyways, silhouettes lined graffiti-covered walls and leaned into archways to whisper conspiratorially with unseen voices.

We were staying in Valparaiso while we waited for Suyai's response. Stranded in Thailand, I sent her the letter knowing she was the only person left who might help us. I didn't know if the letter would reach her, but I asked her to reply to a post office in downtown Valparaiso. As with so many times before, the rest was out of our hands.

The Sunday markets were filling with vendors and springing to life as we crossed the central square. Hole-in-the-wall shops sold fresh bread and sweet *manjar* treats. The post office wouldn't be open until Monday so we couldn't yet check for Suyai's letter. Exhausted from the trip, we resigned ourselves to enjoying a few days of newfound freedom. JC and I walked to nearby hotels looking for cheap lodging while Cody trailed behind us and unsuccessfully tried to go unnoticed. Eventually we found a spartan third-story room with a sliver view of the Pacific Ocean between two crooked buildings.

There are days, and then there are Good Days. The days in Valparaiso were the latter, when we started once again to feel like virile young men, powerful and free and alive. We set up makeshift hammocks in our broke-down palace and opened the splintered Spanish windows wide to inhale the sultry ocean air, breathing in the openness and unleashing rebel yells from the terrace that startled unsuspecting passers-by. We bought liter bottles of Austral beer from a grungy bodega and traipsed through the streets drinking and looking for fresh empanadas, all the while making eyes at pretty Chilean girls. Down by the waterfront, we weaved between the vendors and street performers that filled Plaza Sotomayor with music. Old men in traditional *guaso* attire strummed guitars and sang, and a young girl played a wooden flute. She danced as the old men played, turning in circles as her black pigtails flew behind her like darting tadpoles.

The unknown, the future, came to mean something more than sheer survival.

The next morning I returned to the square and found the post office in a far corner of the plaza, tucked away on a winding side street lined by bright yellow buildings. When the office opened I charged through the door, nearly knocking over a cart of mail.

"*Buenos días, señor.*"

"*Buenos días, joven.*" The clerk peered at me from behind a raised wooden counter.

"Is there a letter for Benjamin Piñera? It would have arrived within the last week."

The elderly man adopted a stern tone. "The letter was addressed to the post office?"

"There was nowhere else to send it."

"Young man, that's not how the mail is supposed to work. I will check but I can't guarantee anything."

The clerk trudged back to the mailroom, grumbling under his breath. He returned quickly.

"Your letter's not here."

"Are you sure? Can you please look one more time? Please. I can't tell you how important it is."

He must have seen the desperation in my eyes, the accumulation of things gone wrong wearing through a thin facade.

"All right. I'll take one more look."

After more paper shuffling, he walked out of the backroom holding a small envelope.

"It was buried under a pile of old mail. You're lucky I was here to find it."

I thanked the white-haired curmudgeon, walked outside into the plaza and tore open the envelope.

March 1, 1973

Dear Benjamin,

> *You boys have a home here as long as you need it. I'll do everything I can to help you. But do everything you can to stay out of trouble. If the Chilean Army finds three American soldiers, you won't be here very long.*
>
> *I've arranged a ride to Santiago for you with a man named Jorge. He's a truck driver who will pass through Valparaiso this Monday.*
>
> *You'll meet Jorge in Plaza Sotomayor at noon on March 3, in front of the statue of Arturo Prat. He is a good man, trustworthy and a comrade in the fight.*
>
> *With love,*
> *Aunt Suyai*

At last, someone would take us in.

Suyai was right to insist that we keep a low profile: gringos in military fatigues were not overly welcome in Allende's Chile, and Cody's blazing blue eyes and shock of crew-cut blond hair would give him away before the first garbled *hola* ever tripped off his tongue. Yet there was something else in the letter that gave me pause.

From friends serving in Intel and chatter in Vietnam, we knew the US was balls deep in fomenting another civil war, this time in Chile. While I knew what Suyai's last phrase signified—*a comrade in the fight*, she had written—I decided not to tell Cody and JC. To Cody, it was a minefield that he needed to avoid, at least for now. And to JC, it was the one thing that could divide us because of the fault lines that ran underneath our family.

We both knew how we felt about Vietnam, but neither of us knew what to think about Chile. In the all-consuming chaos and fear of going AWOL and hiding in Thailand, I was able to push it to the hinterlands of my thoughts, but I always knew it would resurface. That the struggle would come to define our lives more than Vietnam seemed impossible. Yet even after leaving Vietnam, none of us foresaw what would come next.

———————◎———————

The night before Jorge smuggled us into Santiago I dreamed of the last time our family had been in Valparaiso. It must have been '62 or early '63, because my mother was in the dream, and because my father hadn't yet adopted the grim countenance that would later become his trademark.

We were on the beach digging for clams. Mamá stood by a wide pewter vat we brought in the bed of Father's '46 Ford half-ton pickup he bought from a friend at the American Embassy. At her feet was a glistening pile of sunburst yellow lemons that she effortlessly sliced and squeezed into the vat filled with cold water. JC and I dove under the waves that crashed against the rock formations jutting out along the coast, looking for oysters, mussels or *locos* that our family would eat for lunch. The tart lemon juice cooked the seafood, we were told. *How?* I asked. *Porque si, mi hijo,* was the answer. *Just because, my son.* An early lesson that sometimes, Things Are The Way They Are.

As we waded into the ocean a younger boy trailed behind, wanting to be one of the big kids that hauled in the day's meal. We let him follow but warned him not to come in above his chest; we knew of the eddies that formed around these rocky cliffs, powerful enough to pull a man under and pin him down until the sea stole his breath. But we had the invincibility of youth on our side, and in this case, we knew how to avoid the danger. I pulled the goggles over my head, gulped as much air as my lungs could hold and dove down into the sea.

Swimming toward a cluster of rocks, I saw JC descend down a steep rock face, gliding through the water to explore a cove deep in the cliff. I turned over a large rock and peeled two mussels and a clam off the bottom of the ocean. As I pushed the shellfish down into a jute sack attached to my belt, my lungs began to tighten, but I resisted the urge to escape. I relaxed my limbs and succumbed to the peaceful roll of the waves.

The gelatinous push and pull of the current secured me in one enthralling spot just above the seabed, suspended in the soft thrum of the ocean. The waves lapped overhead and my limbs fused with the pendulous rhythm of the water, swaying gently yet secured by the rocking cadence. There I stayed in the stillness, even as the tightness spread outward through my body.

I awoke gasping for breath, besieged by a sharp-nailed tightness in my chest. JC was awake and sitting on his bed. Cody was gone.

"Cody left some time last night, I don't know when," JC said. "He took the rest of the money, too."

"He'll be back," I mumbled. "He may be killing himself, but he would never fuck us over."

We both knew where Cody had gone. To score smack, or at least to look for it. Cody had been the toughest soldier in our company, and as crazy as it sounds, I never worried about someone else hurting him. But he was slowly killing himself.

Cody straggled in just before noon, leaving us barely enough time to meet Jorge in Plaza Sotomayor. If we missed him, we'd be stuck in Valparaiso with no way to get to Santiago other than buying bus tickets, which wouldn't be easy; sympathy for US soldiers on the run was unlikely from the union workers and bureaucrats who would be running the bus station.

"Where have you been?" I asked as he stumbled into the cramped hotel room.

"I was out. Getting to know the city."

His eyes were as wide as dinner plates and embossed with the hollow porcelain shine of a heroin high. Needle tracks traversed his inner arm, which was puffy and red from recent activity. As he aimlessly shuffled around the room searching for a path to his bed, I saw that the left side of his face was bruised and swollen, fat like a rotten grapefruit. I wouldn't have wanted to see what the other guy looked like. I silently thanked JC for insisting that we leave our weapons on the boat. We were already deserters—we didn't need a murder charge pinned on our conspicuous traveling companion.

I looked straight into his lifeless eyes. "In Vietnam, you could be as crazy as you wanted. But now you're our charge, and if you keep using smack we're going to drop your ass in the boonies and leave you to the *Marxistas*."

Cold eyes met my stare. "I never asked you to bring me with you." The words were spit out slowly and maliciously.

"But you came," I said. "If there is one person who is going to make it out alive, it's you."

"Then tell me how to escape this. Tell me your secret. Because at some point over there, I lost my mind."

Those are the words that a soldier can never say. They are an admission of defeat, an admission that he lacked the heart to go on. In the theater of war, they are the words of a dead man walking.

Jorge was a squat and thick-shouldered man with deep furrowed brows, a rotund potbelly and a crooked grin worn wide and generous. We noticed his truck parked in the middle of the crowded plaza before we saw him, an old Chevy cab astride a rusty pre-war chassis. On each side of the flatbed truck were immense wooden placards featuring sprawling facsimiles of Salvador Allende, fist pumping in impassioned oratory.

"I'm guessing that you're Suyai's nephews," he said as he approached.

"That's us," I said. "How did you know?"

"Porque están con el gringo," he answered, laughing.

"You all ready?" Jorge didn't wait for an answer. "Good. *Vamos.* The truck isn't the most comfortable ride, but you guys don't have much of a choice, do you?"

We jogged to keep up with him and tossed the duffle bags over the Allende placard. JC took the front seat and Cody and I hopped in back.

"Hang on tight, boys," Jorge yelled out his window as he sped away, hurtling the truck over potholes. "I'm a busy man and there's no time to waste."

As we climbed the coastal mountains and left Valparaiso behind, Cody sat on his haunches in the truck bed and closed his eyes. He was rubbing the silver St. Christopher pendant that hung from his neck, and I could have sworn that for the first time since I had met him he was praying.

If I didn't know it before, I learned it then: you can end up somewhere and not know how you got there. It was like a hurricane came along and mixed everything up and strew it across the land, and we didn't know where anything came from in the first place. There was no other way to explain such things: Three gringo soldiers fresh from hunting Charlie, a Commie driver and a flatbed truck emblazoned with a socialist hero, caught up together in a Cold War crossfire; two twin brothers with still-sunburned faces and a father who never forgave, caught between two lives that could never coexist.

After a few hours on the open road we approached Santiago and its kingly backdrop, the Cordillera of the Andes. Cody was burnt a violent red from the sun and awoke with confused and clouded eyes. As we entered Santiago we neared La Moneda, the imposing neoclassical presidential palace in the heart of the city. Downtown was bustling as usual, but seemed more frenetic and hostile than I remembered. Several times we passed small-scale skirmishes, teenagers fighting in the street and a young mother with children in tow berating an elderly woman outside of the market. Even the street dogs were agitated and whined implacably on the side of the road.

A group of protesters in crisp white uniforms with black handkerchiefs and red hats was moving north on Avenue Almirante Barroso, marching in regimental fashion down the middle of the street. Swelled by the pride of the pack, they chanted *Patria y Libertad, Patria y Libertad*. New model foreign cars rolled alongside and honked their horns, pumping fists out of car windows and chanting in unison with the marchers.

Jorge veered in front of an oncoming car as we passed the march, swerving west to turn onto a side street.

"*¿Oye hueón, viste? ¿Cachái que ya estamos en plena guerra civil?*" he said as we rumbled past Parque O'Higgins. *Do you realize that we are in the middle of a civil war?*

Suyai and her eight year-old son Salvador lived in Ñuñoa, a working-class neighborhood east of downtown. It was a barrio of faded wooden storefronts, liquor stores and drab low-rise apartment buildings. While far from the wealthiest neighborhood in Santiago, Ñuñoa was beloved by all Chileans because it was the beating heart of the country's passion for the beautiful game. The barrio was dominated by the cavernous Estadio Nacional, the national soccer stadium where Chileans from all walks of life came draped in red to support *La Roja*, the national team.

As we drove through the streets, drying garments flapped overhead on clothes lines and packs of feral dogs guarded city blocks. We arrived at Suyai's house as the setting sun draped a fiery halo over the mountains.

Jorge parked in a dirt alleyway behind a row of dilapidated one-story homes. The row houses had low-slung roofs made of weathered wood planks that bowed inward like tree branches weighed by a heavy snow. As Jorge stepped out of the truck, Salvador burst through the back door and ran to him.

"Jorge! You're finally here!" The boy's bushy black hair bounced up and down as he ran, skinny arms pumping furiously like toy pistons. Salvador jumped into Jorge's outstretched arms.

"Hey, little man. What's going on?"

Cody and I leapt down from the truck bed and our landing kicked up a tumbling dust cloud. Salvador finally noticed the presence of strangers.

"Who are they?" he asked, squinting through the dust.

"They're your cousins. Except for the gringo, of course—I'm not really sure who he is. They'll be staying with you and your mom for a little while."

Standing behind Jorge, Salvador eyed us warily. It was clear by the look on his face that curiosity and fear were dueling for the right to respond. In the end, his curiosity won out.

"Sure, come in. We're about to eat."

JC and I sat down at the kitchen table while Jorge looked for Suyai out front. The floor was made of latticed wooden planks spaced wide enough apart that subtle gusts of air percolated up through the floorboards. On the far wall of the back bedroom was a photograph of a broad-chested man with dark hair, a proud chin and a prominent brow. He was dressed in a factory uniform and holding an Allende flag. A bold inscription on the flag read, *Unidad Popular, Para Siempre.*

The front door flew open and Suyai burst into the kitchen. She looked older than I remembered but she radiated the same palpable affection. Seeing her after so many years brought back a flood of memories: of trips to the beach when she would race down the sand dunes holding our hands, of crashing into the ocean and diving down to the seabed to explore the hidden universe below, and of sitting around the campfire and fighting off heavy eyelids while she regaled us with stories of the founders of the Chilean worker's movement, men and women who fought to secure rights for laborers and farmers. Those stories weren't told until Father had fallen asleep, of course. His response to her uplifting tales was simple, and stern:

The goddamn Communists stole my family's land, chopped it up and parceled it out to illiterate peasants. My family was left with nothing. It was hard to argue because that singular fact was the only one that mattered to him. It was foolhardy to argue against that wrath.

Suyai moved around the house like a listing freighter, her wide hips swinging around corners with unmistakable purpose. JC received Suyai's first bear hug and I was next. Cody was still leaning against the back door when she entered, but he received the biggest hug of all as well as a pair of maternal kisses on the cheek. The room filled with a warmth we hadn't known in years.

"Bienvenidos a Santiago. Que Dios les bendiga y les ampare." That God bless and watch over you.

"Suyai, Cody doesn't speak much Spanish." I said. "I know your English isn't perfect, but could you give it a shot?"

She looked at Cody and gave a playful shrug. "No problem. I speak English well, you'll see. I have been practicing to talk with my nephews. I have waited so long to see you again, *mis queridos*. I always knew you would come back."

"Are you boys hungry?" Before we could answer Suyai was lighting a match to heat the stove. After warming a small cauldron she ladled generous portions of soup into wooden bowls.

"Please, eat as much as you want. It's lentil soup, my specialty. It's time you boys ate well."

After cleaning up dinner and putting Salvador to bed, Suyai finally sat down and rested.

"Is every day like this for you? I mean, this busy?" I asked.

"Yeah, I guess it is. I work as a nanny for a family in Bellavista. You remember Bellavista, don't you?"

"Of course. It's the rich neighborhood full of *cuicos* next to Plaza Italia."

"But it's changing. Even a big-mouthed Commie like Jorge owns property there," she said, laughing.

We had declined to ask about the nature of Jorge's presence in her life.

It was too early, and besides, he seemed trustworthy and willing to help Suyai.

"Whenever I'm not working," she continued, "I'm cooking for Salvador, doing *aseo* around the house or attending one union meeting or another. Then I race back home to put him to bed."

"But he's getting big, isn't he?" she added.

"He's growing like a weed," JC replied. Silence settled in as our thoughts drifted to the past.

"I wish we would have been there when he was born," I finally offered. Even at the age of thirteen, JC and I knew that you show up for your cousin's birth. But Father had refused to go.

"It wasn't your fault. You were just kids."

She looked up at us and willed a tender smile. Right then she looked like Mom, with her delicate features and wide green eyes.

Suyai's bedroom door was still open, and I again looked at the photograph on the wall.

"Is that Cristián in the photo?" I asked.

She didn't even have to look. It was the only picture in the house. "It was. Or is," she stammered. "Yes," she concluded.

"We are so sorry about your loss."

JC's spoke softly. These were the condolences that needed to be said, no matter how much time had passed—the attempts to acknowledge the gravity of the past weighing still on the present.

"Thank you," she said quietly.

Jorge spoke for the first time since we had come into the house. "You and your brother left after the election in '70, right?"

"Yeah. Even though Allende didn't take office until November, Father always expected that Congress would appoint him. It was too risky to stay, he said. We left Santiago on September 12 and landed in Los Angeles the next day."

A flash of anger crossed Suyai's eyes. "Do you know why he wanted to leave right after the election?" she asked.

Herein lay a minefield of half-truths and raw wounds. I knew that if I learned more I probably wouldn't be proud of my father and his work as editor of *El Mercurio*, the largest newspaper in Chile. But I also knew why he did what he did, that it was borne of a deep-seated belief that Allende would ruin the country. I knew that because of the assurance of his hatred.

"He said Chile was no longer safe because of Allende. I always figured it had something to do with his job, but we never asked him directly. You know how he is—it's damn near impossible to talk to him about certain things."

"I do. I know all too well," Suyai said, nodding sympathetically. "But do you know why *El Mercurio* was so controversial?"

"I know it has ties to the *Partido Nacional* and that it opposed Allende and the *Unidad Popular,* Allende's party, in the elections."

"Which is all true," Suyai said. "*El Mercurio* had been a mouthpiece for the *Partido Nacional* and the CIA since '64. But by the '70 elections, it was much worse. The CIA was subsidizing the paper's budget, and many of *El Mercurio's* writers were on the CIA payroll. The paper even compiled lists of Allende supporters to target."

I had never heard such a daunting list of indictments against my father's paper, or against my father.

"I'm sorry you have to hear this from me, but it's the truth. Your father was the CIA's main operative at *El Mercurio* until the day he fled Chile."

JC abruptly slid his chair away from the table and stood up.

"I'm not going to sit here and listen to this. I'll find my own place to stay tonight." He picked up his bag and barged out of the kitchen, slamming the door behind him.

I waited for the door to stop banging before I spoke again. "I'm sorry. JC's been like this since we left Chile. He still blames the Marxists for everything, just like our father.

She crossed her weathered hands in her lap. "You haven't lost him yet. Just keep trying."

But I knew it would never happen. Our childhood was eclipsed by Father's fury at an army of invisible enemies. Being a child in that world was terrifying, and he didn't want to have to remember it. Neither did I, but we owed that to Suyai. At the very least.

The kitchen grew colder as the night winds whipped through the seams in the wall.

"Do you mind me asking what happened to Cristián?"

"No, it's fine. You deserve to know what happened to your uncle."

Suyai looked to the far bedroom wall, eyes searching for the photo. "It was after the presidential elections in '70, when Congress was fighting over who to appoint as President. An Army general kidnapped Rene Schneider, the Commander in Chief of the Army, in an attempted coup. After the attack, the military raided unions' headquarters to neutralize them in case the coup was successful. Cristián was at the union when a tank regiment arrived and soldiers stormed the building."

"No one is sure what happened," she said. "The Army claimed that they were attacked. Shots were fired and three union members were killed."

She gathered herself to finish. "They never even took him to the hospital. They just let him die there."

Tears welled in her eyes as she continued speaking. "The military claimed they had received reports that the unions were arming and would attack if Congress didn't appoint Allende President. But Cristián didn't have any weapons."

Jorge's voice resumed where Suyai had trailed off. "Cristián was my best friend and I know that he'd never hurt a soul. He was a worker, and a loyal man. He didn't deserve to die."

"The coup attempt failed, although Schneider was killed," Jorge continued, "and a few days later Congress named Allende President. Which put a stop to the violence and the coup attempts—until now."

"So what comes next?" I asked.

"No one knows for sure," he said. "We think the military is plotting another coup."

Suyai stood up and paced around the kitchen. "The scary part is not knowing when, or how. We just have to wait for them to do it all over again."

"What will you do if it happens again?"

She replied without a moment's hesitation. "We'll defend the President."

"But how?"

"The people will be able to defend themselves, even if the Army raids every union headquarters. Next time, we'll be ready to fight back. I'm going to make sure of that."

Seeing her anger swell, I realized that even peaceful people can turn violent when they see no other option. I knew that JC, Cody and I could take care of ourselves—we were hardened vets who had faced Charlie down and survived. But if what they said was true, Suyai was in danger, just as surely as Allende was.

After dinner Cody and I rested on the beds Suyai had prepared, improvised side-by-side cots in the kitchen made from old woolen blankets. We fell asleep listening to the wind contort around the creaky wooden home, warmed by full stomachs and a blazing fire. When JC came back the next day, the smell of liquor oozing from his pores, I didn't even bother asking him where he had been. He would have been too angry to talk. Our family mirrored our country, forever fighting itself and unable to forgive the sins of the past.

After escaping a full-fledged civil war in Vietnam, we landed in the middle of a brewing one in Chile. This was the homeland to which we had returned. The Americans had a saying for what had happened to us, a breezy pocket-sized slogan for a real life-sized problem: out of the frying pan, and into the fire. That was us, all right: wayward, and still trapped in the fire.

JC stayed at Suyai's that second night after offering a caveat-laden apology. In the wake of his outburst, we avoided anything resembling political conversation. But independent of politics and Father's past misdeeds, we quickly came to see that our presence would be a financial burden on Suyai and Salvador, one made all the worse by Suyai's insistence on cooking regularly for us. We hadn't eaten well in over two years, she reasoned, and the least we deserved was a few home-cooked meals. Despite the kindness she showed, we needed to find somewhere else to live.

We made the decision to move to Bellavista on our third night in Santiago. Bellavista was a wealthy neighborhood north of Ñuñoa with strong ties to the Catholic Church. The neighborhood bordered Cerro San Cristobal, a soaring mountain crowned by a supplicating Virgin Mary that watched over the city. Although Bellavista wouldn't have been my first choice, Jorge owned a small apartment on Pío Nono, the neighborhood's main thoroughfare, and he offered to let us stay for free for a few months. It was here, among the neighborhood's shady tree-lined streets and outdoor cafes, that we would move into our safe house.

Once the decision was made, Jorge drove us to see the apartment. On the drive, Cody asked: "So where exactly are we going to live?"

JC laughed dryly. "It's the Beverly Hills of Chile."

Eyeing the spacious driveways and stately porticos of our new neighbors' homes, Cody laid his country Bako accent on thick.

"I didn't realize ya'll were such aristocrats."

Yet far from aristocrats, we would be pariahs in our new neighborhood. Cody didn't believe that we would be ostracized just because of our family's politics until Jorge told him he had been blackballed by wealthy neighbors who despised his beliefs (which were advertised in no uncertain terms on his truck's billboards). Jorge advised that we should expect the same treatment. Nonetheless, Suyai and Jorge agreed that this was the safest area for Americans. They joked that all rich Chileans secretly wanted to be gringos. We would just have to forgo hanging the Allende flag, something JC would be just fine with.

To avoid any unwanted attention we returned at midnight to move into the third-floor apartment. We walked through the dim alleyway carting all our worldly possessions in hand, noteworthy more for what was lost than what remained. Weary and bone tired, three young men carried the remnants of a story gone awry: GI shirts, pants, threadbare socks and dog tags; a silver pendant, a mother's ring, a worn Bible; a heroin addiction, a shoulder hole, a crumbling brotherhood and a satchel of debts to pay.

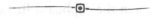

After Allende was elected in September of 1970, my father, JC and I fled to California. We stayed in a two-bedroom bungalow on the outskirts of San Luis Obispo. Those first weeks were hard. JC and I shared a bedroom until Christmas, and the close quarters soon drove us both crazy. Eventually I put an old mattress in the corner of the musty basement, figuring a little privacy was worth living in a cement cave. Father spent most of his time waiting in lines at government agencies to get his name on one list or another, and he was gone for hours at a time without explanation. The social workers that visited were kind but could only help so much. How much could they really do, anyway? We weren't going to become employable or fluent English speakers, no matter how many times they visited. Nobody cared what we had been through, and nothing would come easy.

The days crawled by as we waited for classes to start. We were scheduled to start school in October, which would supposedly give us time to prepare for classes. Those first months were filled with studying, and daily English quizzes painstakingly administered by our father. Although he had no idea if our answers were correct, he badgered us over perceived uncertainties anyway. We spent free time at the beach or watching old television re-runs like *The Andy Griffith Show* and *Gilligan's Island* on a used TV given to us by a relief agency.

American television was ridiculous, but mesmerizing. Everything always turned out for the best no matter how improbable the ending. On *The Andy Griffith Show*, Andy Taylor and his son Opie were the epitome of the America we had heard about in Chile, and the one we were still kind of looking for: simple, old-fashioned and unfailingly virtuous. California circa 1970 was none of those things. *Gilligan's Island* hit a little closer to home, though. It was ludicrous, yet we related to characters marooned on a deserted island and holding out hope for rescue. But deep down, we knew that Father wouldn't return to Chile as long as Allende was President. The man was wasting away in California, too far gone to save.

When we were younger our father was conservative to the point of being puritanical. As for drinking, anything more than a glass of wine was a rarity, and he never touched hard liquor. But in California, bottles of whisky began to pile up in the cupboard in various states of fullness, and his self-control slipped away. The drinking allied with his silence, a sneaking wordlessness that had tunneled down and spread its roots, and dragged the man further away from being a parent.

Our father had always been a serious person—it took a lot to get the man to laugh—but moving to California seemed to conclude a withdrawal that began on that rainy night years ago, when he lost the most important thing in the world, and then started to lose all that was left. There were some days when we didn't exchange a word with him, when it seemed that the only sounds in that house were the screams of words that went unsaid. The tenuous silence was shared between a father, twin sons and a lifetime's worth of grudges and ghosts.

The holiday season arrived, but we hardly noticed. While the rest of the nation celebrated Thanksgiving, we ate greasy Chinese food and tried to understand the origins of the holiday. *So they celebrated with a feast after surviving a winter thanks to the natives' help, and then drove them off the land?* While Chile had its own sordid tales of indigenous treatment, we failed to see a reason to give thanks for a bounty reaped at someone else's expense. It was just one more custom in our new country that we didn't understand.

Christmas came next, and we found ourselves penniless and unprepared for the opulent gift giving. While other families welcomed distant relatives and went to Christmas Eve mass, JC and I went to the library and then to the beach to play soccer. A couple of surfers asked to play and we started a pick-up game, and we came home after dark. On the walk home, we could see families smiling and laughing around Christmas trees through candlelit windows. Our own house was dark and boarded up, an eyesore on the genteel neighborhood.

Walking through the front door, whisky musk filled the house, extending its sweaty stench high and low in the old bungalow. The light in the kitchen was turned on, and we heard the scraping sound of a bottle being pulled across the kitchen table. JC headed for his room and closed the door, muttering in disgust.

A dress shirt from the day's job search lay wrinkled over a kitchen chair. Leaning back in his chair, Father was holding a tall tumbler filled to the brim and staring vacantly out the kitchen window.

"Are you all right?" I asked.

He nodded and took a gulp from the glass. His crisp black hair was normally combed neatly to the side and secured by generous amounts of pomade, but that night it hung low and disheveled over his forehead, obscuring his eyes. I had never seen him so drunk before.

He took one more lengthy pull from the tumbler and then looked up at me. "Why do you think this happened?"

"Why what happened?"

"Was it all just bad luck? I can handle if it's my fault—hell, it probably is—but the fact that she was killed by *them*? It can't just end like that, with nobody to blame."

"But it did. We don't know where that bullet came from. We never will."

The old man sighed, waved me off and returned to his drink. No sooner had I entered his world than I was dispatched. When I left the kitchen he had resumed his blank stare out of the window.

I didn't blame him, not then, not for everything. Certainly not for Mom being hit by a stray bullet at an Allende rally, fired amid the chaos of a shootout between Allende supporters and right-wing protesters. More than one shot was fired that rainy night, the police told us later, but she was the only one to die. More importantly, the police never identified who fired the bullet that killed her. Still, my father was convinced that the Marxists had killed his wife, and from then on he would know only revenge. JC and I were ten years old and ignorant of the politics. We just knew she was gone.

Freckled brothers with sunburned cheeks left with an angry Half Father; twin-faced boys who lost their Moon and their Sun.

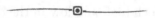

Suyai knew a huge network of Allende supporters, union officials and party apparatchiks in Santiago. Visitors arrived at all hours of the day to debate politics, sharing news of rallies and furnishing intelligence around the small kitchen table. One frequent visitor was the editor of a small newspaper called *La Voz del Pueblo* that I met a week after we moved to the apartment. JC decided not to come, grumbling something about there being too many Commies for his liking.

When she introduced me to Ricardo she told him I was one of the nephews that had moved to the United States, the ones she always talked about.

"He has grown into such a good young man. I wanted you to meet him. I'm so proud of him." Thankfully, she omitted the part about me deserting the US Army.

Unruly white hairs poked out capriciously from Ricardo's bald pate and thick eyebrows. He looked like a tall friendly elf.

"How well do you speak English, son?"

"Fluently, sir. I learned it when we lived in California."

He raised his hand to his chin and calmly appraised me.

"Are you interested in a job? We need someone who can monitor foreign news outlets and translate stories that come in over the wire."

"Yes, sir. I've been looking for work."

"We don't pay very much but you can work every day. Shifts are in the afternoons and evenings, after writers submit their copies. You can also help run the printing presses at night."

"Yes, sir. I won't let you down."

With that, I began my career in the newspaper business. I started the next day at the humble newsroom in Ñuñoa, working in the shadows of the Estadio Nacional. I never envisioned what a fateful decision taking that job would be, how it would open my eyes to what was happening in my country. And how it would eventually bring me face to face with it.

The newspaper industry is a strange beast, full of unwritten rules and customs that I had to quickly learn. Even at *La Voz del Pueblo,* a small daily broadsheet where each journalist had to crank out multiple stories to cover the day's news, there was an entire universe of communication independent of the words that went to press. The most difficult part was learning to understand a story's angle based on what the writer chose to omit. On my first day, Ricardo had said, *You'll learn more by paying attention to what they don't say than what they do.*

Weeks of rationing beans and rice had me considering heading down into the copper mines for a paycheck, so when Ricardo offered me the job the answer was simple. As for working at a paper, though—that was luck, pure and simple, because I had always loved to read and write. And now I'd get paid for it.

As a boy I grew up reading classic South American writers like García Marquez and Vargas Llosa, storytellers whose characters seemed so adventurous and quixotic as to be otherworldly. They painted a South American mural of vivid colors and unabated passions, a land of deceit, nobility and redemption. Our own childhood was more somber and regimented, imbued by political warring and the dark presence of the military. A home used for covert military meetings is not all that conducive to a lighthearted upbringing. We never received an introduction to these men, and we thought it normal that generals would come to the house late at night, speak with Father in hushed tones and leave unmarked packages. Nor did Father ever explain the reason for the meetings. We just assumed it had something to do with his job, and instinctively believed that whatever he was doing was correct, as children are wont to do. We also assumed that it had something to do with the godless *Marxistas* that he hated so much, but we kept those suspicions to ourselves.

Memories of *El Mercurio's* downtown newspaper headquarters were murky. Those memories were tinged by a vaguely threatening coloration, a sense of seriousness and gloom. I did remember my father once meeting an imperiously dressed Air Force officer in his office, a furtive man with a severe widow's peak and an ugly black mole on his cheek. Standing rigid as a statue in my father's office, the man wielded an aura of authority and violence. These were my father's colleagues and confidantes, men who would become notorious years later. Men who would change history.

In 1973, Chile was not lacking for headline news. Every day heralded a new and frightening twist in the struggle for power, and *La Voz del Pueblo* was in a unique position to cover those events. The paper was smaller than the major Santiago dailies and remained unaffiliated with any political party, officially or otherwise. This position afforded more independence than that of the government-run papers, providing some cover to criticize the official party line. And unlike *El Mercurio*, we weren't on a foreign intelligence agency's payroll, freeing us to report on disloyalty in the armed forces and the growing presence of foreign influences. This independence didn't bring in much profit, but it did carve out a narrow space to tell the truth.

The journalists of *La Voz del Pueblo* worked tirelessly to report the real news. To say it was an uphill fight was putting it mildly—Chile was a playground for deception, a potent mix of blind righteousness and hatred of those with different beliefs, and the ends would always justify the means. Allende's enemies didn't have to invent examples of foreign influence in Chile: The KGB funded Allende's '70 campaign and made cash payments directly to the President to secure his support. Allende, a natural ideological ally of the Soviet Union, in turn provided the KGB with political information. From the other side of the planet, Nixon had long ago ordered the CIA *to make the Chilean economy scream*, and the agency had been collaborating with various right-wing political parties for more than a decade. The CIA also provided weapons and support for the Schneider assassination and the aborted coup attempt that ensued. There was no shortage of ammunition for those looking for shocking newspaper headlines.

I followed closely on Ricardo's heels those first few days in the newsroom as he issued rapid-fire commands and worked the phones. Watching him, I quickly learned journalism—good journalism, at least—requires an exacting attention to detail and a heightened bullshit detector. I didn't really understand the need for that skepticism until Ricardo first asked me to draft an article based on a report that came in over the wire. It was my first week on the job.

Parliamentary elections had been held the previous week and Allende's party had increased its power in Congress. The wire report emphasized the US government's respect for Chilean sovereignty and featured Henry Kissinger stating that Chile's fate belonged to its people. Feeling a sense of relief at the news, I read the wire several times and then began to translate it to Spanish. The literal translation was difficult, but I had soon completed a first draft.

I walked into Ricardo's office and placed the article on his desk. "I've finished the draft." He nodded, placed his glasses on the arch of his nose and picked up the article.

After less than a minute he stopped reading and peered at me over the thin wire frames. He couldn't have read more than half of it.

"When you were in Vietnam, did you hear the speech Allende gave at the UN General Assembly?"

Hearing my darkest secret voiced so cavalierly was sickening.

"How did you know?" I asked timorously.

"Don't worry, son. I just figured it out. Your aunt's vagueness about where you had lived. The sudden arrival in Chile, when you're also American citizens and should be able to return there. And Cody. Why would you all come to Chile? I suspected it right away."

"Does anyone else know?"

"No, I promise. What confirmed it for me was the look in your eyes. There was a wariness there, like you had already seen a lifetime go by."

He paused a moment and calmly folded his hands on his desk. "Trust me. Your secret is safe with me."

I worked to quiet the fear brewing inside and returned to his question.

"I did hear about it. We had a friend in Intel who had been supplying us information about Chile for a while—since I began to consider it as an escape route, really."

"What did you hear?"

I paused and looked at Ricardo, unsure of how much to trust my new boss. "That Allende blamed the US for Chile's problems, and that he was a Soviet agent."

"That's all?" Conversations with Ricardo often went like this, with him prodding for more information and testing versions of the truth.

"That was it."

"Did the story say if Allende's claim was true?" The cigarette between his fingers emitted a blue trail of smoke that twisted up to the ceiling.

"Was it…was it true?"

"Yes. Did the news say if it was true?"

"No. It only said he was blaming the US because he was a Soviet agent."

"Well, at least you heard part of the story. Allende does have close ties to the Soviet Union and Brezhnev, though the only real economic aid Chile received was tied to arms purchases."

Leaning forward on his elbows, a mischievous smirk unwound from the corners of his mouth.

"So, the story you heard didn't mention that Allende called Chile 'a silent Vietnam?' Or that the US has funneled millions of dollars into black ops, misinformation and propaganda?"

His voice wasn't sarcastic, just matter of fact, and he continued with the same tone.

"Or that the Chilean military has sent hundreds of anti-Allende officers to Panama to train with the CIA, and purchased arms from the American military? Did you hear any of that?"

Confronted with my own ignorance, I offered the only answer that came to mind. "They didn't mention that."

Ricardo extinguished his cigarette in the ashtray, shuffled out from behind his desk and put his hand on my shoulder.

"I don't blame you for not knowing the whole story. The truth is a rare commodity these days."

Ricardo paced over to the wide bay window in his office. A group of boys were shouting and playing soccer in the narrow back alleyway. "The mark of a good journalist is one who writes the real story, whatever that might be. No matter what the consequences."

"I promise you," he added, "there are people out there spewing their lies as God's truth, and it's up to you to see through it. Otherwise you're just another one of them."

"Yes, sir." As he returned to the papers on his desk I turned to leave the office.

"Remember, son," he said as I reached the doorway. *"En el país de los ciegos, el tuerto es rey."*

His were words of wisdom, and warning. *In the land of the blind, the one-eyed man is king.*

As the news that came across our desk became even more offensive to the facts on the ground, the job became all the more difficult, and all the more important. If only to avoid being One of Them.

The weeks rolled by, work at the newspaper filled the days and nights, and time seemed to reclaim its forward march. But nothing else about our refugee lives returned to normal.

Events in Chile were a series of small battles devolving into intractable wars, with radical politicians standing by to fan the flames. It was heartbreaking to see so many Chileans led astray by the various self-anointed leaders. The UP used the controversy as an excuse to push the agenda of its most radical factions, calling for the expropriation of industries and the arming of partisans. Shopkeepers hoarded food and supplies to protest Allende's reforms, only to see their incomes decimated and their neighbors go hungry. Many Chilean miners went on strike, forcing Chile to suspend foreign copper exports and crippling its main revenue stream. *El Teniente*, the nation's largest copper mine, nearly shut down in July of '73, and while many of the strikes were financed from outside Chile, it's unclear if the striking miners knew where to collect lost wages. Truckers parked their vehicles in empty fields and parking lots, grinding food supply chains to a halt. It was our job to report these stories to a country that often didn't want to hear them.

The most aggravating part of the job was watching foreign propaganda run verbatim in the papers as if it were legitimate news. The audacity of these stories was matched by articles from *El Siglo* and other pro-UP outlets that parroted the government line and promised a socialist utopia. Like class notes passed between gossiping schoolchildren, the underlying reality of the event was found only in the aggregation of the data points, shreds of truth found between the lines of shrewd and self-interested versions.

Under Ricardo's watch I came to view the work as a daily battle of wits. Would I fail to understand the angle behind the story? Would I miss an important fact that exposed a wire as Soviet propaganda or CIA tradecraft? My goal, simply put, was to not be the fool. My only weapons in the fight were my reason, my will and the facts at hand.

The litany of distortions and mistruths that came across the wire was hard to stomach. But there was one day, April 2, when I hoped for something better. That was the date, nine years earlier, when my mother died. I hoped some force of cosmic justice would reign, if not for Chile, then at least for her. But sitting down to review the day's stories, it was clear that would not be the case.

Two articles stood out among the day's news. The first recounted a massive rally in Santiago the previous day:

"Emotiva Despedida a Obrero José Ahumada"
(Emotional Goodbye to Worker José Ahumada)

At a worker's rally, a man named José Ahumada had been struck by a bullet fired into the crowd. This murder, like the one that killed my mother, remained unclaimed and unsolved. The article recounted how a crowd of thousands had come together to honor Mr. Ahumada and to hear President Allende's eulogy.

Missing, its absence staining the pages with unabashed prejudice, was any mention of who was responsible for the killing. No mention of suspects, or a police investigation, or even of the probable reason he was killed. No one was responsible for this murder, we were told. Just bad luck amid the backdrop of a lawless government.

The second was an article placed in the early pages of *El Mercurio* by the *Partido Nacional:*

"¿Hasta Cuando Los Comunistas Se Amparan En Los Militares?"
(How Long Will the Communists Seek Refuge in the Military?)

The article claimed that the government and General Bachelet were abusing the obedience of the military through its program to distribute food to hungry neighborhoods. The piece failed to mention any of the conditions that had created the food shortage, such as shopkeepers hoarding food or the trucker's strike. The article concluded by urging citizens to oppose Allende at every step.

From the deserts of Arica to the frigid savannah of Punta Arenas, there was a northern wind descending on Chile.

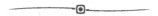

They moved in unison, the Communists. Schools of people casting about like minnows, guided by an unseen force that drew them to the next protest, the next strike, the next checkpoint on their revolutionary timeline. When they moved they flowed liked a flood crashing over levees, absorbing everything in their path and carrying it along with them. Maybe there was a rule engraved somewhere on an old socialist scroll that solidarity meant never leaving home without comrades. Or maybe they had learned long ago that there is safety in numbers, and long odds on going it alone. When they amassed, be it standing or walking, the whole lot of them jumped up and down as if skipping rope. They chanted in rhythm, hypnotically— *El que no salta es momio, el que no salta es momio*—accusing anyone not jumping of being a right-wing mummy.

The *Partido Nacional* marches were much the same, packed with zealots chanting and brandishing anti-Allende flags like weapons. There was anger in those marches, anger that would not be sated without carnage. Any crossing of paths between the two militias was destined to end violently, with blood in the streets and revenge lingering in the air.

There was one exception to the rule. For some reason, the two sides were able to coexist anytime religion entered the mix. Whether it was a

Sunday morning walk to church or the annual eighty-mile pilgrimage to the Sanctuary of Our Lady in Lo Vásquez, an unspoken ceasefire was observed in all matters ecclesiastic. The pilgrimage was without question the most amazing part. The annual ceremony saw Santiaguinos march mile after mile in the central valley to reach the hillside grotto. Thousands of people who hated each other just a day before extended an olive branch for the hours-long trek to worship the Virgin Mary, and then promptly withdrew it upon their return.

One day when Suyai and I were downtown we came upon a right-wing *Patria y Libertad* protest gravitating toward La Moneda. Awed by the collective rage of the protesters, I asked Suyai why the *Marxistas* and the *momios* couldn't set aside their anger long enough to coexist for even an afternoon unless God was there to mediate.

"We may not trust each other, but we do trust in the Lord," she said. *"A Dios rogando con el mazo dando." Pray to God and keep your powder dry.*

Not that I had any right, but that was my gripe with Him—that his watch was unreliable. There were places where he didn't venture, and no one would convince me otherwise. Vietnam was one of those places, where I watched men coolly torture others as naturally as they would prepare breakfast, and men took to killing without a second thought, and sometimes without a first. It was better to tell yourself that God wasn't there, because the alternative was that he was there, and just didn't do anything about it.

Cody spent the lion's share of those first weeks sleeping at the apartment. After waking up in the afternoon he would patrol the streets for a cheap meal and a cheaper bottle of booze and then return to hibernate. In those early days, his presence was a mystery. Despite his size, he managed to disappear in the background, hidden somewhere behind a bewildered silence and his own broad shadow. Jorge had lent us a small TV with antler antennas and Cody would sit slumped on the couch, eyes heavy and glazed, and watch Chilean shows that he didn't understand. Maybe that was the idea.

For as long as we had known Cody, he had been different. Amid the hipness and gaudy wealth of the California coast, he was a throwback, a good kid with uncommonly pure intentions. For all that he was—a gun-toting country boy from a broken trailer home and a reckless drunk who would fight anyone, anytime—Cody was loyal, a junkyard dog who never learned the self-serving rules of adulthood. He had looked out for us in California and helped us survive that confusing and alien world. We owed it to him to help him survive this one.

It was Cody's nature to keep things private and the horrors of his withdrawal were no exception. I never once heard him complain about what was going on inside his body, even when his eyes were bulging and he was maniacally scratching his arms and legs. I knew little of addicts, but I did know that they were susceptible to temptations just like the rest of us. Only their moments of weakness had the power to destroy lives, all over again. The only good thing was that he didn't know anyone in Chile and had no way of buying smack. For a little while, at least.

Trouble was, I didn't have much time to keep an eye on him. I was working night and day, exhausting twelve-hour rotations piling on top of each other like bricks. The dusk to dawn shifts stole most of my nights, and the gentle hum of the printing presses came to substitute for sleep. It was comforting, though, the purposeful lack of sleep. After years of suffering through sleepless nights, of hearing ominous sounds that never were and chasing a running-wild imagination back into its cage, there was finally a reason to be awake. The familiar circling of the conveyor belt and the soft pressing of ink to paper were far better than whatever dreams might come.

All those days and nights of work were beginning to pay off. The knowledge passed on from Ricardo and the older printers had made me into an able pressman, capable of running and repairing the mercurial machine almost as well as the veteran mechanics. Ricardo had even complimented my progress as a journalist. I was learning how to be something other than a soldier. Who knows what could happen? Maybe I too could be a newspaperman, a full-time truth teller, if given the chance.

One weekend in late May a Sunday night shift bled into late morning. Dog-tired and stained with black smudges from loading delivery trucks, I returned to the apartment through a crisp winter morning, exhausted and content. Coming home after working through the night left me with a floating feeling, free to sleep the day away having paid my dues. After a long sleep I would wake in the late afternoon and wander the streets looking for a meal and a cold beer. Later, when the night approached, I was ready to explore while the rest of the world slept.

The workweek had begun in earnest. Sleepy-eyed *nanas* took crosstown buses to prepare breakfasts for families that hadn't yet woken up, and yawning factory workers with frayed work boots and sack lunches rode crowded trains, resting their eyes while their heads vibrated on cold windowpanes. When I finally arrived home I sat at the ceramic kitchen table and surveyed the apartment. Dishes were piled a foot high in the sink, and the marigold ashtray on the table was filled to the brim with blackened cigarette butts. I hadn't seen Cody in a few days. Instead of the usual ruckus that filtered through the walls of his room there was silence. JC was also nowhere to be found. Just days earlier he mentioned that he'd found a job for a legal organization I'd never heard of. When he told me about the job he was maddeningly vague, but I let it pass. As twins, we had already shared so much without ever choosing to, and we both understood the need to keep some things to ourselves.

As boys, we were unalarmed by the blurry osmosis that all too easily melded us back into a single identify. But Vietnam had carved out much more than it ceded, and the space between had widened. The boundaries had become firm and the borders uncompromising. Sometimes I knew him less than a stranger.

I lit the stove and waited for the water to boil. After emptying the last of the coffee grounds into a mug, I added the steaming water and sipped the weak coffee.

Where do we go from here? It was a question without an answer. We had little money and we had deserted the Army during wartime. If we were lucky we would spend a few years imprisoned in military barracks. The dark specter of confinement, though, would be too much for both Cody and I. After Cambodia, neither of us would ever allow ourselves to be imprisoned. I would have rather died than be caged again. There was still no way out.

Footsteps clanked against the winding metal staircase behind the apartment. There was a brief struggle with keys, muttered cursing, and then Cody plowed through the door, nearly tripping over his own feet. The smell of stale booze overwhelmed the small kitchen.

"Damn, late night *hueón*?"

"I guess so." He shuffled in through the doorway, eclipsing the space with his lumberjack frame.

"How long has this sleeping-all-day, drinking-all-night thing been going on? What are you doing out there?"

A low, monotone voiced rumbled forth. "I mostly just walk around the city." He brushed past me, sat down at the table and stared impassively out the window.

"You want coffee?" I asked, offering him my cup. No response.

"Cody, I don't understand. What do you get by wandering around the city all night? Are you banging *putas*?"

Almost imperceptibly, he shook his head side to side.

"I'm still waiting," I said.

"You already have an escape," he answered. "You work through the night. JC, you know how he is. He acts like we didn't just spend two years of our life in the jungle, and that deserting the Army is no big deal. I can't fake it like him."

Leaning back in his chair, he closed his eyes. "I've got no way out."

"I can help you," I offered futilely. "How can I help you?"

I would have asked him why he wasn't sleeping if I didn't already know. For a GI who had served in country, the nighttime was a playground for fear. Imagination was unwelcome, because the ability to conjure up something worse than that reality left no space to breathe.

"Cody, are you using again?"

Before answering, he thought for a few moments. "No. Not yet. But it's the only way I know how to feel better."

After our dinner conversation I went to bed and slept a dreamless sleep, too tired to think about how to pull Cody through the escape hatch.

Santiago was founded in 1541 by a conquistador and an army of horsemen with steel swords and visions of riches in gold-glinted eyes. Pedro de Valdivia, the newly crowned Spanish Viceroy of Chile, decided to build the city between two branches of the Mapocho River, in a valley surrounded by prodigious mountain ranges, to utilize the region's formidable natural defenses. As it turns out, de Valdivia's fears were not unfounded. Despite his best attempts to assure nearby Mapuche tribes that his army had come in peace, the Spanish lost a small measure of credibility when they enslaved *indígenas* to work in gold mines, thus provoking the ire of the locals. It was then, after that failed overture of peace, that the wars began.

First came the three consecutive years of warfare starting in the spring of 1541, when half of Santiago was razed to the ground and any Santiaguinos not killed in battle starved, or nearly did. The seasons of war returned when the Spanish army pushed south to the Bio-Bio River and trespassed too far onto Mapuche soil, and yet again years later when the Mapuche raised an army and sacked Fort Tucapel. When de Valdivia and a small contingent of cavalry gallantly rushed to defend the fort, the Spanish were slaughtered and the Viceroy was captured. Unfortunately for the Viceroy, there was no deification of white Europeans in this remote corner of the world, only post-battle ceremonies to consume the strength of vanquished enemies. As legend has it, de Valdivia had his quivering heart ripped out and eaten by Mapuche warriors.

Unlike the Incans and Aztecs, Mapuche society did not comprehend the concept of slavery. As a people, they simply could not countenance becoming slaves, servants or even subjects to the Spanish Crown. Even after losing entire armies, the Mapuches waged guerilla warfare as they retreated, all the while training new warriors and preparing for the next attack. Their only course of action was to continue fighting, forever, or until the foreigners left their land. Whichever came first. Long after the more opulent New World natives had fallen to Spanish muskets and cannons, the Mapuches fought on. They were pushed off their land, only to reclaim it by rising up and destroying Spanish settlements south of the Bio-Bio. They would repel foreign armies for nearly three hundred and fifty years, a struggle spanning centuries of Spanish colonial rule and decades of a sovereign Chile.

Yet somehow, despite the ever-present incursions and reprisals and the seeking of retribution, Santiago never fell into enemy hands. The ancient Spanish stronghold ensconced between the skyscraping mountains and the Mapocho's wide river branches remained under firm *criollo* control. But while Santiago remained protected from outside invaders, the Spanish founders never realized that a city could be safe from without but destroyed from within.

Protected from afar, this was when their sanctuary would turn against them: when the giant earthen plates below the mountains convulsed and tore the city limb from limb, and when the rushing rapids of the Mapocho rose above the riverbanks and exploded over, washing away homes and the people inside them like ants in a rainstorm. Long after the warring tribes were killed off or marched away to distant reservations, the mountains and the rivers still wreaked their havoc. While trying to protect against outsiders, the city's tragedies emanated from within.

This was our refuge, a city safe from everyone and everything but its own self-immolation. It was 5,000 miles away from Washington, Capitalism, and 9,000 miles away from Moscow, Communism, a country at the end of the world that could never get far enough away from itself.

My favorite part of Santiago was a few blocks south of the apartment, a stretch of side streets lined with cafes and student bars near Universidad Católica. The outdoor tables edging up to the road were always full, and the boisterous roar of conversation could be heard blocks away. I often went there to drink and watch the people pass by. There, for a few ephemeral moments, I felt a sense of normalcy. Just another unworried face in the unworried crowd.

The boy was a rag-tag prodigy, a one-man drumming machine well shy of manhood but with the wizened bearing of a *caudillo*. I first saw him at the corner of Bernardo O'Higgins and Santa Lucia, but he would appear in patios and plazas around the neighborhood. He played day and night, easily logging ten-hour workdays, and more on weekends. Once upon a time, Cody came with me to drink and watch him, but those visits dwindled after he began to frequent Parque Italiano looking for smack and disappeared for days on end.

The boy's act captivated the entire block. Strapped on his back was a miniature bass drum festooned with colorful base pedals, and there was a cymbal affixed to the rim of the drum. Tied to the base pedals were white shoelace chords that stretched to his feet and fastened into his shoe eyelets. He held two drumsticks like inverted ski poles, and with inward turns of the wrists beat a top-line rhythm with drum tips made of bounded cotton. The base pedals and cymbals were played by stomping, twirling feet. The boy danced and played in perfect time, a thrashing warrior heralding his charge.

He was a charming kid, with a wide smile and a God-given grace, and he played with a skill and fortitude clear to even a casual observer. That he was *indígena* was obvious at first glance—the simmering eyes, black hair and aquiline nose clearly displayed his roots. That he was poor was also just as clear, a poverty revealed by dirty clothes and a dusty face.

The hardest part of watching him was when he finished his performance and politely begged his wages. Some observers gave him a few pesos, others just a smile, and either way the boy moved on without incident. But he was also rebuffed by more than a few scornful looks. Then came the shame, and the downcast eyes, and the dissolution of pride. Then, begging alms with an outstretched hand, he was knocked down to size, a maestro pleading for spare change.

A child like that, working for a living in a roughed-up life, didn't deserve anyone's scorn. Those people that looked down on him sat on empty thrones, presiding over an order that no longer was and never should have been. They didn't understand that sometimes, there is more honor at the bottom than the top.

The amber sun streamed in through the windows and turned the apartment into a monsoon, leaden and humid. Judging from the commotion in the street it was already afternoon. The creaky bay window that opened onto Pío Nono had been left ajar and joyous child shrieks danced breezily through the cobblestone streets. That Sunday was my day off at the newspaper, my first in weeks. After working the Saturday graveyard shift I usually slept in, but never this late; the heavy work schedule was grinding me down. When I walked out of my room, still half asleep, JC was rustling in the kitchen. The raucous slamming of drawers and cabinets forced me to yell above the noise.

"Are you hungry?"

"Yeah, I'm starving."

"Do you want to go find something to eat? I'm sick of *porotos.*"

As we walked south toward Plaza Italia, the streets were full of children running around in their Sunday's best. Pig-tailed little girls in flower print dresses raced ahead of their families, clinging with petite fingers to their father's much larger hands and excitedly pulling them through the crowds. The early bird drinking juntas seated underneath kodachrome parasols called their meetings to order and cracked open the day's inaugural bottles of pisco and beer.

We sat down at a small café and ordered the cheapest beer on the menu. With the widespread food shortages, printed menus didn't count for much, so we asked the waiter what was in stock. *Porotos*, was the answer. And *pan*. Our earlier vision of juicy steak was just one more illusion of which we were disabused. We ordered the beans and bread, hoping for a slice of butter on the side.

We sipped our beers and stared vacantly at the passing crowds. Watching JC's eyes wander through the passing crowds, I noticed how much older he looked. A knot of worry had formed on his brow and age lines spread out from the corners of his light green eyes like river deltas. For identical twins there were a lot of incongruences between us—he was a little thicker in the shoulders, I was slightly taller, and JC alone had inherited my father's serious mouth and parsimonious smile—but I imagined that I looked to others much like he looked to me, a young man growing old before his time.

"Did you see that the Gringo Congress cut off funds for operations in Laos and Cambodia?"

"I did," he answered stiffly. "A little too late for us. You both were lucky to make it out. You were lucky Cody was there." JC's voice trailed off.

"I know, I know. He's not doing well, you know..."

"Yeah, I noticed."

"We need to help him. He needs a job, something to do. Maybe a chance to get out of Santiago."

JC positioned his blank gaze over my shoulder. "What more can we do? We dragged him out of Vietnam, smack addiction and all, and are putting him up for free. Now he drinks, sleeps and wanders the streets at night. God knows if he's found a dealer."

"I know he's struggling. But we owe him. Listen, I've been thinking— what if we take a road trip? We'll go south, to Patagonia. Get him away from the city."

JC gulped down the rest of his beer and thumped the table with the empty glass. "Fine, I'll go. But I don't think anything is going to help him."

The road trip was an idea I had been thinking about for a few weeks, since I began to dream about our old family trips to southern Chile. I hoped it could undo some of the damage, but I feared that JC had already given up on Cody and would be unable to forgive his weakness. That was the darker side of brother, coarse and unforgiving, just like our father. Deep down, I knew it wasn't all JC's fault. If Mom had been around just a few more years, things would have turned out different. She would have softened the raw edges and bandaged them for the journey ahead.

After eating, we walked back to the apartment in silence. JC assaulted the air as he walked, his forceful gait inflicting blows on imaginary foes.

"I'm still hungry. The stores don't have any food. Even the goddamned restaurants don't have meat. What the hell is going on in this country?"

I hesitated before answering. Did he really not know what was causing the shortages, or was he looking for an argument? The trap was too facile, the straw man too phony. It was an old trick Father employed when the villain was already marked in his sights.

"JC, you know why there's a food shortage. Shop owners are hoarding their supplies to make the government look bad."

"Do you really believe that? If you do, you're as ignorant as the Marxists." His was a *mecha corta,* a short fuse, and he was quick to blame— another trait inherited from Father.

"Where do you think this is coming from? This crisis is a ploy to create chaos. I don't claim that Allende knows anything about how to run an economy, but you know there's a secret campaign to ruin this country."

He hadn't listened to a word that I had spoken. "You are believing their lies."

"And you're refusing to accept the facts, because it would mean that you're wrong, and that Father was wrong. You can't blame them for everything. And you can't blame them for Mom."

"You'll see how this turns out. And then you'll be sorry."

Another open front in the metastasizing civil war, ignited between two brothers. Our own ember to add to the spreading wildfires. But he was right about one thing. I would be sorry. We would all be sorry.

I can't begin to tell you how things changed after we first arrived in California, when we became part American and witnessed the marvelous spectacle that is the United States. Everything worked—the schools, the buses, the trains—and it worked well. There was no more waiting in endless lines to buy basic groceries at the supermarket only to find that bread, flour and salt were sold out, and no more waiting for hours at a bank only to learn that your account was frozen. There was no more wondering when your country would collapse under its own weight. We had arrived to the land of plenty, a place of riches and decadence that we would never fully comprehend.

We met Cody in November during our first month in high school and quickly became friends. He was honest, funny and courageous enough to befriend displaced twins without caring what others would think. Soon thereafter he was pushing to take a road trip. He wanted to get out of San Luis Obispo, to *just go somewhere,* almost as bad as Father had wanted to get out of Chile. Winter came and went, because none of us could take time off from work. We finally decided that we would go to San Francisco over Spring Break.

We saved every penny we earned bussing tables and scraped together enough to hitchhike our way up the California coast. The last leg, passing small seaside towns south of the Bay, was made with a hippie trucker who chain smoked joints and veered his big rig wildly between lanes. The pony-tailed driver took advantage of the captive audience, recounting his late 60's glory days when the earth stopped spinning on its axis and harmony reigned in the Golden State. JC and I listened for a short while and then tuned him out. Cody never bothered to pay attention in the first place. The trucker was passing through San Francisco on his way up the coast to

Seattle, carrying signs and banners that would be used at a war protest. We all shared a skeptical glance. What kind of company paid for their truck drivers to deliver protest signs? But we let it pass. *Don't bite the hand that feeds you*, my father would have said.

We arrived in San Francisco at dusk and asked to be dropped off at the first landmark that came to mind, Golden Gate Park. We jumped out of the big rig, crossed the street and entered a huge open space that spanned for miles. In the middle of the park there was a palatial marble conservatory crowned by white flowers. As the sun went down, swarms of people converged on the downtown park, and the entire park was filled with kids that were laughing, drinking and smoking joints.

Cody's friend had recommended we stay in Haight Ashbury, which was next to the park. We found a rundown motel with burnt orange carpet and an air conditioner as loud as a plane engine, but it fit our budget. We threw our meager luggage on the floor and descended on the bars. JC and I were only eighteen and Cody seventeen, but we didn't have a problem getting past the bouncers. Cody led the way, a six-foot-three colossus with mountainous shoulders and conspicuously brutish strength, and the bouncers let us pass without a second look. We started at the Gold Cane, a crowded dive bar in the heart of Haight Ashbury.

"Here's to hitting the road," Cody said as he raised the first shot of whisky.

"And here's to America," I shouted above the barroom clamor. We clanked our glasses together and downed the stinging shots.

We drank until the sun came up, roaming from bar to bar and talking to every girl we crossed, armed with the invincibility of youth. The women were all over Cody, as usual. But the night was alive, and JC managed to sweet talk some pretty southern girl into the backroom. Later on at a dive bar in the Mission I crossed paths with a darling little *chiquita* with smoky eyes.

"*¿No eres de aquí, cierto?*" Her breath was sweet on my neck as she sidled up next to me.

I laughed nervously. "No, I'm not. *Soy de Chile.* I'm here with my brother and our friend to see San Francisco."

"I didn't think so. Me either." She was small and beautiful, with wavy dark hair and a playful smile.

"Where are you from, then?"

"Los Angeles," she said, and then smiled. "Mexico, actually."

Her name was Marisa. We danced and laughed all night, and left when the bar closed to make our way back to the hotel, drunk and happy and holding hands like children. Neither Cody nor JC had returned.

We spent the night together in a rickety hotel bed, the raucous San Francisco night and the ocean air accompanying my first night with a woman.

In San Francisco, liberated from our father's grasp, we felt the intoxicating pull of a still-to-be-formed future. We jumped on cable cars and smoked joints on roofs and cajoled bums to buy us booze and chased pretty girls into smoky bars. We strolled up and down the polychromatic hills and dales and watched the great American theater play out in impressionist hues, distinct dots and colors emerging into a sensory consciousness recognizable only upon stepping back to view the entire panorama.

Marisa was with me the entire time. I held her hand as we jitterbugged through the beatific streets high on the thrill of lust and limitless possibilities and what was yet to come. Later we fucked, and then made love, unaware of what to call it but knowing that we were tasting and breathing moments of raw electrifying romance. In San Francisco, for the first time in a long time—since two twin-faced boys ran through cool drops of honey rain while their mother watched over, when memories were foggy and sweet and bursting at the seams—for the first time since our worlds were torn asunder, it felt like Things Were Going To Be All Right.

Even then I never expected to see her again. We fully expected to be in Vietnam before the year was over. But even though that was the last time I saw her, the time together was real. In my darkest moments in Vietnam, when the fear and death and all-consuming cynicism became too much to bear, I thought of her and dreamed of the day when I would feel that again. The memory was a bridge back to the real world, and a reason to keep fighting during the most hellish times. It was the possibility of taking a pretty little thing by the hand and going somewhere, anywhere, with a pure heart and fire in the belly; it was the remembrance of watching fireworks paint celestial strokes on a midnight pallet as we drank whisky and understood brotherhood, and just maybe an infinitesimally small part of the cosmos. It was possibility that kept me alive, and impelled me to get us out of Vietnam.

In Santiago, our runaway life slowly crumbled, piece by piece. Steadily losing Cody was hard to bear. Ravaged by heroin, he was a mere shell of the magnetic force we had known in California. But losing JC was harder, not just because he was my brother, but because I had no idea how to fix it. Since those first few days in Valparaiso we had barely seen each other. Even when we did cross paths we exchanged cursory nods like vague acquaintances.

I worried that I would never be able to reach him again, and I worried that I couldn't change his mind anymore than I could change my Father's mind. Whether the hatred or the loss came first, I never knew, but Father blamed the Marxists for the death of his wife. No matter how unjust the verdict, vengeance naturally ensued, and seeped down to impressionable minds below.

None of us knew who had fired that bullet. It could have just as easily been one of the fanatical *milicos* who turned out that day to oppose Allende. I have tried to accept that I will never know who killed my mother. JC, though, like Father, would never forgive them. The loss of a wife and mother carved out a hollowness that could never be filled, like the bullet hole in my shoulder. For that, forgiveness was impossible. But JC did ultimately forgive me, in a way infinitely more powerful than any words ever could.

In our mother's eyes we were twin boys that could do no wrong, innocent even when we did awful little-boy things. She was a proud mother and completely in denial about the trouble her boys stirred up.

From the outside, identical twins are a novelty, a genetic anomaly that miraculously produces two gurgling look-alike babies instead of one. And it's only natural to treat them as a single entity, a package deal. But if everyone else treats two people the same, it just makes them try all the harder to be different.

Brothers usually fight. It's just how they're programmed. But JC and I never fought each other, at least physically. After Mom was gone and Father became an apparition of his former self, we relied on one another too much—fighting isn't an option when it's you against the world. Being so protective of each other helped mask the differences between us, but those differences couldn't be covered up and stashed away forever. As we grew older and adjusted to life without her, the differences piled up and pulled us apart because she wasn't there to hold us together.

Our mother used to tell a story about JC and I when she talked about her boys, which happened in nearly all of her conversations. When we were little, around age five or six, I was convinced that JC needed glasses. Although the doctors would predictably report that his vision was 20/20 at his annual checkup, I knew something was wrong, and I could not be dissuaded. I knew he needed glasses because there was no way he was seeing the same things I was seeing. We would witness the same set of events, but our mom would hear two very different accounts of what took place. Sometimes it had to do with disputes between us, but other times it was just recounting something we had both witnessed. We had Story One, and Story Two, and no credible reason why they were so different.

I knew that I was telling the truth, so I reasoned he must have had vision problems—he just wasn't seeing what *actually* happened. Where he saw fair, I saw unfair. Where I saw white, he saw black. *He just needs glasses,* I would tell our mom. *It's not his fault he can't see what happens.* A half-blind brother who couldn't quite get the story right.

Looking back now, he probably thought the same of me. But he was always quiet, more apt to suffer something rather than confront it. I tried to fix it. I'm not sure either of us ever really understood it. We became young men, and we became who we are. And at some point, we segued from a life animated by the possibility of the unknown to one grounded in the stark reality of the known. I don't know when it happens. But I do know that it does. And while it becomes a part of the lives swirling around us, it is a change that occurs deep on the inside, known only to ourselves.

———————————◎———————————

It was a Friday night and I had nothing to do. JC left and didn't say where he was going, and Cody's door had been closed all day after two nights out on the streets. I worried about him, and I was angry with him, but I couldn't stop him. I understood the impulse to self-medicate even if I didn't approve. As for me, I was broke and lonely, so I made the hour-long walk to Suyai's house looking for company.

I often visited her on Friday nights, although I usually let her know I was coming ahead of time. Assuming Cody wasn't strung out, he would join me. While he hardly spoke during the visits, it was clear he wanted to be around a family and to feel some semblance of normalcy. Suyai treated him like another nephew, lavishing him with affection and home-cooked food.

By the time I arrived it was already past sundown. The back alleyway was empty except for a truck parked behind the house. The windows were unlocked but the back door was propped open. Walking toward the back door, I saw a shadow scurry to the bed of the truck, pick up a bulky case and then disappear back into the house. I picked up an ax handle leaning against a neighbor's door and slowly crept to the back door.

With my back against the side of the house, I heard men murmuring inside the kitchen.

"Put them underneath the bed in the back room." It was a gruff voice that I didn't recognize. I steeled myself for close quarter combatives, recalling my Army training: close on the enemy, engage and disarm with blows to the hands and feet, and then quickly debilitate with rapid strikes to the chin, neck and eyes. A blow to the larynx was the most efficient finishing move. I had killed men in Vietnam using these techniques.

I sidled around the corner and spotted a dark figure carrying the case into the kitchen. I stomped the back of his knee to force him on the ground and raised the axe handle, aiming for his throat. As I began to swing the axe, I heard a voice that I immediately recognized.

"Benjamin! Stop! Don't hurt him!"

It was Suyai. She was standing in the front hallway holding a pile of rifles in her arms like logs of firewood. I froze and let the man drop to the floor.

"Suyai! Are you all right? Who are these men?"

She rushed over to help the man I had attacked. "I'm sorry, Marcos! It's my nephew. He's just trying to protect me. He didn't know."

The man slid away to the wall on his backside and glared at me.

"What the hell is going on here? What are you doing with all these guns?"

"*Oh, mi'jito.* I didn't want to involve you in this," she said, helping the man to his feet. "I'm helping to bring weapons into Chile."

"But what happens if the Army catches you?"

"They won't. But you can't tell anyone, especially not JC. Just act like you were never here. OK, *mi amor?*"

"I won't. But please, be careful."

Walking toward the kitchen door, I looked back at Suyai. She had returned to piling the rifles underneath her bed.

"If you're in danger, please tell me. I can protect you," I said as I walked out the back door, the familiar sound of clattering rifles echoing behind me.

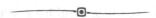

When Father was in California he took up a number of different hobbies, in part because he had little else to fill his days. While he never had a lot of friends, he hardly spoke to anyone after we were *exiled*, as he called it. Of course, both JC and I knew that we weren't exiled—Father had left because he feared for his life, not because the government forced him to leave. But we let him maintain the charade to avoid an argument. *I just want to be left alone*, he said. By and large, we honored his request.

One of the hobbies that actually stuck was pottery. He bought a used potter's wheel and began to try his hand at the craft. After some spectacular failures and a few raging outbursts when his frustrations were unleashed on misshapen dishes, he started to improve.

Creating earthenware that will withstand the test of time requires a delicate balance. On the initial revolutions around the wheel, when the clay is still wet and amorphous, every piece is basically the same. Soon, though, the potter begins to shape and mold the clay into something distinct and identifiable. They craft a base of a certain size and shape, and walls of a particular curvature. With time, the potter's hands create a singular pattern of ridges and grooves that are ingrained into the solidifying work.

The potter then arrives at a decisive juncture, when they must fully and faithfully render their vision before the clay hardens, or risk an unformed product. But they also must stop before it becomes brittle and crumbles after excessive manipulation. Striking this balance to create a strong yet supple piece is the potter's greatest challenge. Father struggled mightily with it, and even after years of practice never fully mastered the art.

On those rare occasions when he would open up for a few moments and talk with me—in his own cautious, roundabout way—I would try to ask him some of the lingering questions that were never far from my thoughts. What Mom was like when she was alive. Where the rest of our family was in Chile, and if they were safe. And what was next for the three of us.

But I also wondered about his pottery. What can be done if the design needs more time, more molding and shaping, yet is already hardening into a final form?

I never really got answers to those questions, or any others, before he disappeared back into his workroom and his resolute silence.

The trucking strike that began in October of '72 progressed in fits and starts through the summer of '73. The strike had converted parking lots into auto graveyards, with vehicles aligned in crooked rows and columns like unruly platoons awaiting inspection by their CO's. But for the truckers who refused to join the strike, it meant more routes and more pay, and they worked day and night to transport basic necessities to the far corners of Chile. Jorge was one of the drivers who kept on working. The extra work carried him up and down Chile's beanpole thin terrain, and near the end he was covering nearly half of South America.

Suyai invited Jorge and me over for dinner that Friday night. I was coming alone because Cody had gone missing, again, and JC said in no uncertain terms that he would not be visiting our aunt any time soon. It was true that she inhabited a different world than we did, one filled by marches and union meetings as a front-line soldier in her worker's revolution. But she was still family, and had offered us a lifeline when our father refused.

At dinner, Jorge was as friendly as ever. "So how is your gringo friend doing?" He was fascinated by America even as he detested its meddling in Chilean politics.

"Not so well. Actually, we were hoping to take him on a trip. Is there any way we could hitch a ride the next time you head south?"

He laughed and shook his head in amazement. "You boys haven't had enough traveling as it is?"

"We need to get out of Santiago. We just need to get away."

To get away. It didn't occur to me then that to get away is the same as to escape. How many times could we escape? Whether it was fate, or will, or just dumb luck that had kept us alive, I didn't know. Surely it would run out, though. What happens when there's nowhere left to run?

Jorge was set to depart on a long haul south to Punta Arenas, one of the most southerly places on earth outside of Antarctica. Suyai recommended he drop us off near Coihaique, in the Aysén region, before the mountains bowed and flattened into windswept plains. Coihaique was a small town deep in the heart of Chilean Patagonia, nestled among towering peaks and waterfalls that trundled into brave country lakes. It was said, simply, to be the most beautiful place on earth.

JC worked late the night before we left. I had just learned that his new job was with a law firm owned by Pablo Rodriguez, a leader of *Patria y Libertad*. Rodriguez founded the fascist paramilitary group in '71 to oppose the UP, and its legal activities included organizing protests against the government; its extralegal activities included spying, propaganda and murder. JC was working for people that would gladly kill Suyai and Jorge if given the chance. It was a betrayal, but I didn't know how deeply it went, and this trip was not the time for us to battle. A war can take many forms, and Cody needed a break from all of them.

Driving south through Patagonia, Jorge stopped only a few times to unload deliveries. When we reached Puerto Montt we patrolled the town to look for supplies, as it was the last city for hundreds of miles with provisions. Then we boarded a southbound ferry, and for the next six hours endured the unyielding sways of the Pacific.

We arrived in a small port at the northern edge of Aysén and then began our descent into Patagonia. We were traveling south on the one and only path that ran through the wild frontier, the rocky *Carretera Austral*. Jorge would drop us off in Puerto Bertrand, a village on the stately banks of Rio Baker, and one of the last outposts on the route. From there we would hitchhike north to Coihaique to meet him in a week's time.

Once we reached Patagonia we began to hitchhike, rattling along the country paths, hypnotized by the soaring peaks, emerald hills and frothing waterfalls of the noble land. It didn't take more than a few hours for the mystique to cast its spell, and the fog that had enveloped Cody for the past year began to lift. He even forgave us for searching his bag and throwing away the heroin he packed. Cody said it himself: anger was unworthy of Patagonia, too small and petty for such a place. If he was suffering from withdrawal, he was doing a hell of a job hiding it. The awe in his eyes was the same as in ours, replacing the vapid heroin sheen of the past year.

That first night we camped downstream from a series of rapids on the banks of the Rio Baker. River rapids create shallow grooves where trout can rest and feed without fighting upstream currents, and are often the best fishing spots along a river. We chose the campsite because JC had managed to scrounge together a length of fishing line and a hook back in Santiago, and there was a slow eddy near the riverbank where trout were jumping to feed on insects. Using the line and hook we crafted a crude fishing pole from a cypress branch and then went to work trapping flies near the riverbank to use as bait. Once the makeshift pole was set and the hook was baited, JC cast the line in the water.

"Watch the master at work," he joked.

Despite his intense focus, JC spent an hour casting and re-casting without any success. In time, the sound of his mumbled curses grew to an audible level. After JC gave up I tried my hand, and for nearly an hour I whipped the line over the river's surface, dropping it down momentarily on the water to imitate a fallen insect. I employed all the tricks Father had taught us but still failed to lure a single bite. It was growing dark and our stomachs were grumbling. I was sure we would go to bed hungry.

"Let me try," Cody said, standing in the shadows of the tree line that approached the river's edge. Elevated by the steep slope of the embankment, he looked like a giant.

"Good luck." I said, unable to hide the doubt in my voice. While Cody had grown up hunting and fishing, he had never fished the Baker, and I was sure he had never used a tree branch as a fishing pole. The sun was falling behind the mountains and a crescent moon was forming in the sky. The fish would stop feeding soon.

Cody waded slowly into the glacial waters and began to cast the line slowly and methodically, free from the hurry that had overtaken me. I wished him luck and wandered down the bank to a cool patch of grass. Lying down under a grove of cypress trees, I listened to the rustling river and felt my eyelids grow heavy.

JC let out a surprised yelp that echoed through the countryside and startled me from sleep.

"You've got one!"

Looking down the river, I saw JC running to the banks. Cody was thigh deep in the eddy, deftly feeding line through his guide hand.

"JC, calm down," Cody said patiently. "He'll give me a good fight. This is gonna' take a little while."

As I ran to the bank, the trout exploded through the water and soared above the river. She was a beauty, a rainbow trout with a shock of pink bending along her spotted body. Cody was beginning to pull the line in more forcefully and the trout was slowly giving up the fight.

"Empty my Army sack," Cody said calmly. I obliged and handed him the empty bag. With one hand holding the line, he dragged the rucksack through the water and netted the night's dinner.

We ate like kings that night and every night after thanks to his fishing prowess. I couldn't help but think that this was how Cody would be if he had just had a normal life—a happy-go-lucky guy with a hearty laugh, without a care in the world. Just a regular kid.

Three days later an elderly farmer picked us up on the roadside and drove us to Puerto Tranquilo, smoking a pipe with one hand while he deftly navigated the twisting road with the other. Hours later he dropped us off at a driveway a few kilometers south of town and told us to walk down the winding path until we hit a bluff where we could camp. We trekked down the steep hill and arrived at a small wood cabin overlooking

Lago General Carrera, the largest lake in Chile. We paid the friendly grandpa a few pesos and pitched our tent in a grassy opening on the cliff.

While JC and I started to build a fire, Cody ran up to the cliff, stripping off his clothes as he ran, and launched himself into the crystal lake below.

"No way he just jumped off that cliff," JC said, shaking his head in disbelief. "He is one crazy son of a bitch."

When we reached the edge of the cliff we saw Cody swimming in the freezing waters below. "Come on in, boys," he yelled. "The water's warm."

Stripping down to our boxers, we followed his lead and jumped, our howls ricocheting off the cliffs and reverberating through the canyon.

Through the initial fog of the freezing water I could see a marble rock structure near the cliff and swam toward it. The silver, black and turquoise formation rested precariously on top of thin spiraling edifices. As we swam through the marble caves the cold sank its claws in deeper, but we continued through the shadowy tunnels. Soon the cold overtook our bodies and we swam for shore, shivering and content.

"This place is amazing," Cody said later as we sat by the fire and passed around a bottle of pisco. "It's God's country."

The next afternoon we met two sisters in Puerto Tranquilo who were driving north to camp. After a round of flirtatious entreaties they agreed to give us a ride. We all camped on a lake at the base of the mountains, and Cody ended up using the few Spanish words he knew to convince the younger sister to take a midnight swim with him. We heard him promising a bottle of pisco that we knew he didn't have—we had polished off all our liquor the night before—but hell, he had to get her away from the older sister somehow. I drank red wine, laughed and gazed at the stars.

When Jorge picked us up in Coihaique's central plaza two days later, I knew instantly that something was wrong. He looked tired, and he barely said a word.

"Jorge, did something happen? Is everything all right?"

"Well…yes, yes, everything is fine."

I had never seen him like this. "Well, you seem worried."

Jorge stared straight ahead, motionless. I thought he was ignoring the question until he started to speak, very slowly. The words seemed hard for him to pronounce.

"Congress declared the Allende government unconstitutional."

"What does that mean? What will happen now?"

"It means that Congress supports a military coup. Now more than ever we expect a *Golpe*. This may lead to civil war."

Patagonia quickly became a distant memory. As we moved farther north I avoided waking Cody, and even when he finally awoke I couldn't look him in the eye; I couldn't lie to him, and I couldn't tell him the truth.

It was early morning when we got back to Santiago. Jorge had told JC and Cody the news when I was sleeping. Cody jumped out of the truck and started walking down the street, headed straight for Plaza Italia. JC and I stood on the porch and waited for the other to say something.

"There's no turning back now," I said. "There's going to be a coup."

"I know." He looked out over the empty street. "But this is what needs to happen. It's for the good of the country."

"How can you say that? Why not just wait for the next election like Chileans have been doing for generations? No matter how bad this president has been, the alternative will be much worse."

"How would it be worse?" he asked.

"JC, it's a military attacking its own people. It's a massacre. How can that be a good thing?"

There was no answer forthcoming. He wouldn't even look at me. I knew that in his mind that didn't make me right, though. Even after so many years we were still looking through a mirror image, him on one side and me on the other. And somewhere in between, the world was inverted.

"You'll never understand," he finally said. "You just can't."

He was right. I would never understand.

"Remember," I said. "No matter what happens, I'll always be your brother. Your blood."

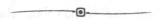

Ñuñoa, the barrio where Suyai and Salvador lived, had always been one of the rougher neighborhoods in Santiago. Young men lined the streets after dark drinking and harassing outsiders, and muggings were not uncommon. Rumors also occasionally circulated about stabbings, or even shootings. Stories about women being attacked were less frequent, but even Suyai feared certain streets after dark. She still braved those streets, though. *I refuse to give up this neighborhood*, she said.

The neighborhood had become even more dangerous since Suyai and Cristián had moved in a decade ago. As he got older, Salvador spent more time running the streets with older boys, and Suyai worried that he would become just another *pandillero,* drinking and thieving. Especially because his dad wasn't around to set him straight.

"I won't let them get to Salvador," she told me. "I won't let him give up."

Suyai and our mom grew up poor, the children of *campesinos* from Southern Chile who migrated to Santiago to work as laborers and servants. Suyai had worked every day of her life and she wasn't about to offer excuses for anyone. *No matter what's going on around you,* she told Salvador, *you can always make a choice.*

Just a few blocks north, an aging warehouse had been torn down and new homes were being built on the city block. While the area was a long way from a ritzy neighborhood, it was safer than the streets near the stadium where Suyai and Salvador lived. After a few of her neighbors moved to the block, Suyai decided she and Salvador would move, too. Like most of her neighbors, Suyai was not wealthy enough to buy a new home. But she wouldn't need to, because of an old Chilean tradition called a minga.

Originating on the island of Chiloé, a minga is an event when a community helps one of its own with a difficult task. Oftentimes, mingas were held to transport a house to a new location. To honor the community's contribution, the recipient of the help would throw a party for the community afterward.

The house would be hoisted onto a massive pallet made of felled tree trunks and then pulled to the new location. There wasn't a chance in hell of moving anything made of concrete or steel, but the method worked surprisingly well for small wood cabins, the typical Chilean home. What was unique about Suyai's minga is that instead of hauling the house through farms and fields, it would be dragged through downtown Santiago. But Suyai didn't get too hung up on decorum.

The actual move lasted only a few hours. The house was lifted with the help of Jorge's flatbed truck, a pair of oxen supplied by a neighbor and the straining muscles of dozens of neighborhood men. Halyard ropes normally used on freighters were tied between the tree trunks to hold the pallet together, and men on each side guided the house through the streets. An advance guard led the way, stopping traffic to allow the hulking contraption to rattle past, and children ran behind the procession, hopping with excitement at the day's commotion.

Back in Suyai's old neighborhood, Patagonian lambs were already roasting over an open fire and old women wearing wool shawls stirred pots of sweet corn stew and cooked empanadas over glowing coals. After the house was moved, the crowd migrated back to the wafting aroma of the *asado* and feasted on the mountain of grilled meats. The lot was filled to the brim with neighbors hovering around the fire and trimming off pieces of fire-roasted lamb from the spit. It was a feast for princes, served to the people.

A grandfather who lived next door sat on a crumbling rock wall and strummed folk songs on an old guitar. As the music grew and expanded into the fading evening light, young women flocked into the street and began dancing in a circle, hands clasped together. The girls' red and purple dresses shimmered in the flames, a merry go-round of fluttering braids, whirling skirts and smiles that illuminated the minga in a warm glow. I turned and scanned the crowd looking for Suyai but she had disappeared into the swirling mass of people.

When I turned back to the fire, a blur of braided pigtails laid a teardrop kiss on my cheek. The girl's back was turned, but I could see she was delicate, with slim shoulders and a graceful neck. She wore an orange and red dress the color of the sun.

"Oops!" she cried playfully as she turned around to see who she had bumped into.

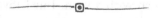

Do you recall when you were a child and you learned the most important thing in the world? When you experienced the tenderness of caring for a child, or the pride of providing for a family? When you came to know something so basic that you wondered how you ever survived without it?

I was meant to love a woman. This woman. Ayelen. Light caramel skin glowing in the moonlight, with a lightning bug smile and eyes as wild as the moon.

"It's all right," I said. She flashed a contagious grin and resumed her place in the undulating swirl of dancers. I waited for her to come around, wondering what to do next.

I never understood where I found the courage to pull her out of the circle, push the strands of silky hair off her forehead and kiss her. I don't believe I was thinking anything, really. Just a young man who knew a simple thing.

The good thing in my life was Ayelen. She made up for all of the bad and allowed me to forget the rest. Being with her made the rest of time seem like a colorless preface until I could see her again. Yet the rest of the day served its purpose, creating a time and space to wait for her. We spent every possible moment together, enduring any and all inconveniences to steal seconds from the day.

Our relationship had to remain a secret to her parents, though. She had told me very little about her family other than to reveal that her dad headed a union syndicate, and that he had a nasty temper. She never said that he hit her but I could tell she was afraid of him. I told Ayelen that I would protect her, but she was more concerned for her mom's safety than her own. Although her parents had heard gossip about the minga and her father, a bilious man who headed a powerful union syndicate, was angered by the neighborhood rumors, we still saw each other most nights because she told them she was working extra night shifts. It was a necessary mistruth, we reasoned, because it allowed us to be together.

Ayelen had never been with a man. But I loved her and she knew it, and that drove her to break the rules she had lived by all her life. Before we were together, I didn't really understand why she trusted me with her innocence, even asked me to take it. But after, I knew. I learned that a time comes when you need to be closer to someone, closer than childhood lives allow. She would come to the apartment and we would listen to American rock and roll and make love, and then drink wine on the steps of the back porch, spellbound by the velvet hem between the mountains and the sky. In those hours we could ignore the dark echoes from downtown.

The days ran together in a pearl string of laughter and intertwined hands and stolen kisses, of drinking too much wine and making love deep into the night, and again in the softness of morning. To her, the reality of it was only starting to come into focus, but for me it had always been clear. Maybe it was spending so much time away from civilization and being deprived of the calming influence of a woman that readied me to settle down at a young age. Never a believer in the mythology of true love, I tried to rationalize where the sensation came from. But there was no reasonable explanation.

What more can I say about Ayelen. I learned that her name meant both to give thanks and to smile in Mapudungun, the language of her mother's parents, and that she spent her days helping others do both. We spent every waking minute together, and we slept with tangled limbs to be closer than in waking life. I ceased to dream without her. I loved her, and it transcended the quotidian notions of affection or lust or duty. I loved her without thought or remedy.

Walking through Bellavista one night after dinner, Ayelen was strangely quiet. As a matter of habit she chose her words carefully, but she had hardly said a word the entire night. I asked her what she was thinking about.

"I'm wondering what it's like to have lost a parent. Is it better not to have one, or to hate one that you have?"

The question surprised me. "I don't know. Do you hate your father?"

"When he hits my mother, yes. I hate him then. I hate him enough then that I hate him a little all the time." Voicing this admission pained her deeply.

"But you didn't answer," she said. "Which do you think is harder?"

I searched for the honest answer, and the response came slowly.

"I don't know. I only know that my life would be unrecognizable if she was still here. And that I would give anything to have her back, just for one day. But it's been so long."

My God, was that true. We were just little boys when she was died. There was so much I would never know about her.

"Time makes you forget," I said, "no matter how hard you fight it. It dulls colors and blurs edges. And what hurts the most is that you even forget the time you had with them. Death can steal the past, too."

I woke up the next morning and looked out the window at a smoggy white sky. Santiago was buried under a thick fog that crept up the mountainsides. To the east, only the highest Andean peaks were visible through the filmy screen, jagged icebergs levitating on a sea of mist. When I turned to look at Ayelen, she was propped up on her elbow.

"Good morning, *preciosa*," I said.

"Good morning."

"So is this going to be a regular thing? I wake up and you'll be staring at me?"

"Maybe."

"How did you sleep?"

"Good. I dreamed about you."

"About what?"

She laughed softly and curled her arm under mine. "You. How you just appeared in my life, out of thin air. Does it even seem real to you?"

"Does being with you seem real to me? Yeah, it seems real to me. Is it not real to you?"

Instead of answering right away she mulled the question over, taking little care to hide her feelings. She was anachronistically sincere.

"You're real to me," she finally said. "You, here now, in front of me. This day is real. But your past, where you've come from? How can it be real when you won't talk about it?"

"Trust me, you don't want to know. I just want to spare you from what I'm trying to forget."

I pulled her closer, relishing the warmth of her body as she curled into me. "Things are getting better because of the people in my life here," I said. "You, and Suyai and Salvador. I have family here. I want to leave the rest in the past."

"If this life is going to be real for me," she said, "then there can't be parts of you that are off limits. It has to be everything. Then it will be real."

She already knew me inside and out, knew me so well that I shouldn't have bothered trying to keep anything from her. But there are some things that get buried so deep that they can't be found no matter who is looking.

Ayelen had been a soccer fan since childhood, something she picked up from her dad. Fortunately we supported the same team, La Universidad de Chile, which helped avoid what would have been a sore spot between us. As a loyal *Chuncha*, it was inconceivable that she would miss the biggest game of the year against La U's archrival, Colo Colo.

"I would love to go," I told her when she showed me the pair of coveted tickets. "But I have to work that day."

"Ay, *pobrecito*. You'll have to call in sick. We're not missing the *Super Clásico*." The issue had been decided, and was not up for debate. The girl was one of a kind.

We left for the stadium two hours before game time.

"Tell me again why we have to leave so early?" It was the first game I had attended since I was eight and I was a little rusty on the protocol.

"There is no such thing as a reserved seat in Chile. If we want to sit close, we need to get there early. We probably should have left an hour ago."

My question made her realize just how out of place I was in this homeland of mine that had come to feel so foreign.

"You really have become a gringo." She laughed and caressed my cheek with her fingers. "Just make sure you don't start to dance like one."

Although the lead time seemed excessive, it became clear why we had left so early as we neared the stadium. Fans were streaming in from all directions and converging like a samba line, singing and dancing and drinking their way into the stadium. From the side we entered, the fans were all *Chunchos* waving red and blue flags. Chileans knew not to approach the stadium from the opponent's side; those who entered with the other team's *barra* would be lucky to escape with only bumps and bruises.

"Just wait until we run into the Colo Colo fans outside the stadium," she said. "That's when this gets interesting. Keep an eye out."

Allegiance to a *barra*, a team's group of fans, wasn't really a choice. It was based on your neighborhood and your family's heritage, with bonds that stretched back generations. Switching allegiances just wasn't done.

Passions and emotions naturally ran high, and fights and projectile bottles were common occurrences.

It was a brisk sunny day, the kind of winter afternoon warm enough to lure people outside for a few hours before the evening winds drove them to seek shelter. Our seats were in the front row, mere steps away from the field. As the game surged back and forth, Ayelen and I stood with our arms around each other, sipping beers and cheering in the middle of a sea of crazed fans.

When La U scored the first goal of the game near the end of the second half, our section went crazy. An older teenage boy sitting next to Ayelen jumped up wildly and threw his arms in the air, dumping his beer on her lap in the process.

"Watch what you're doing!" she yelled at him.

"Fuck you," the drunken teenaged leered.

"Don't talk to her like that."

"Fuck you, too. Nice accent—where are you from, anyway? Stupid gringos."

"Don't do this. Just sit down and shut your mouth."

"*Concha tu madre, culiao.*" As the teenager leaned forward to confront me, he bumped Ayelen and she fell back into her seat.

Above all else we are creatures of habit, doing what we've done because it's what we know to do. Instincts make decisions before our minds have time to assent. The Army hardwired certain instincts in me, and they were irreversible.

I deflected his wide-swinging punch and slammed my fist into his throat. The drunken teen crumpled to the ground gasping for breath. His friend lunged at me with a wild right hook. I dodged that blow and leveled him with an elbow to the temple. The second teenager fell on top of his friend in front of Ayelen. The other fans watched, stunned and speechless.

"We need to go. Now." Ayelen grabbed my arm and pulled me into the aisleway, down the asphalt tunnel steps and through the nearest gate. I had never seen her so angry. Her hands were balled into tiny fists.

Outside the stadium, the wind was blowing cold gusts. Ayelen walked with her head down to deflect the chilly streams of air.

"I'm sorry," I said. "I was just trying to protect you."

"Did you do that because you were drinking?"

"Of course not. I did it because he shoved you."

"You shouldn't have. If that's how you act when you drink then I don't want to be around you."

We continued walking toward her house. As we neared her street, she stopped and turned towards me.

"What's going on? I don't get it."

She took a deep breath to collect herself. "You have to understand, some of my best memories are from when I came to games with my dad. We would come early and drink hot chocolate, and on cold days he would wrap a blanket around me."

Her voice trailed off as her thoughts drifted to another time and place. "And he stopped taking me when he started drinking. After that, games meant he would come home drunk and angry and take it out on my Mom."

"I'm sorry."

"You know, in a way I'm actually grateful he stopped taking me," she said. "I think he was trying to save me."

"Save you from what?"

"Even then, he knew he was fading farther away from the man he used to be. I think he was trying to spare me from seeing him like that."

"But if he still cared about you, why couldn't he just be a good father instead of a drunk?" I knew the question might hurt her, but we had promised each other honesty, even when it hurt.

"I don't know. I just think that some people try, and fail. They can't be the person they're supposed to be, but they still keep trying to be that person, in smaller ways."

"But he can't go back and be a good father to you. He can't undo what he's done."

"No one can. But blaming someone for the past helps about as much as wishing for a different future—you can try all you like, but it's not going to change anything."

We construct fortresses around What Happened, and try to convince ourselves that those times and places are guarded, that they are protected from the prying eyes of the present. And they are safe, and they stay hidden, and everything is all right, until the walls come crumbling down and what was hidden is exposed in plain sight. And the most damning thing is that you ever tricked yourself into believing they were safe in the first place.

Santiago was a ticking time bomb. People talked openly of a military coup d'état in the streets, and those in favor of a *Golpe* spoke excitedly of newly promoted generals that favored military action. Meanwhile, Allende supporters grew more wary with every new report of military raids or paramilitary attacks, raids often aimed at unions and workers.

On May 26, the Chilean Supreme Court took the extraordinary step of declaring that Allende had acted unconstitutionally, citing his refusal to allow the national police to counteract his administration's economic reforms. Tellingly, the Court had conspicuously less to say about the constitutionality of the previous coup attempts. On June 5, Chile was forced to suspend foreign copper exports because production from state-owned mines had been crippled by the ongoing strike. On June 21, *El Mercurio* was closed for six days by the government for inciting a massive strike that led to violence, gunfire and bombings, an order that was later rescinded by the courts. Shortly thereafter, the military launched its first coup attempt against Allende.

On the morning of June 29 the thinly veiled façade of a peaceful opposition was shattered. A tank regiment led by Colonel Robert Souper surrounded La Moneda and the Ministry of Defense and proceeded to open fire on the government buildings. Mutinous army officers that planned the coup had been exposed the previous day, and after news of the coup was leaked Souper hastily gave the order to attack. In response, Allende ordered that loyal elements of the Army confront the insurgent tank regiment and asked citizens to be prepared to *fight alongside the soldiers of Chile*. Troops loyal to Allende arrived minutes later.

The night of the Souper coup, the printing press' plates were misaligned and we spent three hours in the dead of night fixing them. After repairing the press, the day's papers began to whiz through the creaky machine, fresh black ink glistening coolly on the pages.

We knew immediately when the *Tanquetazo* began. Even from the newsroom in Ñuñoa we could hear the brusque sounds of tank and small arms fire coming from downtown. I bolted outside and began to run toward La Moneda, fighting through the seething crowds.

In the plaza, people were tending to the injured bystanders. One young woman crouched in a corner as a young boy and an old man lifted her up and screamed for help. She was holding her hand over a stomach wound that spewed blood onto the dusty sidewalk.

In front of La Moneda, near a tall Chilean flag flapping violently in the main square, a man in full military regalia approached the first in a long colonnade of tanks. As he walked toward the tank he held his arm outstretched, ordering it to halt. In his other arm he held a Thompson sub-machine gun.

"I am General Prats, your Commander in Chief. I am ordering you to dismount and surrender," he said.

General Prats fixed his gaze on the unmoving tank turret and waited. Moments later a soldier propped open the hatch. The young man jumped down, surrendered his pistol and saluted. After the soldier was taken into custody, Prats continued down the line, ordering and securing the surrender of soldiers from the rest of the tanks. As he approached each tank and waited for the soldiers to dismount, the entire plaza watched in silence, afraid to make a move that might upset whatever tenuous equilibrium was preventing all-out war.

When he reached the last tank, he again ordered their surrender. A soldier stood on top of the tank brandishing a machine gun.

"I will not surrender!" the soldier shouted. A pained expression washed over General Prat's face.

"Dismount and surrender. You are betraying your country and disobeying direct orders from your Commander in Chief." General Prats stared down the barrel of a rifle but spoke calmly, with an avuncular firmness. The standoff dragged on with neither man flinching.

Suddenly a lieutenant appeared from behind the tank, held a pistol to the young soldier's temple and arrested him, ending the crisis. As the line of rebel soldiers was marched away in handcuffs, they all stared at the ground, unable to look at General Prats.

These were the sparks of war. I knew war, more intimately than those baby-faced soldiers, and I knew they had no idea what would come next. But they were simply following orders, as I had done so many times before. Marching blindly into the abyss and dragging a country with them.

All the running away had led us nowhere. And any time we fled, what we left behind caught up in due time and left nowhere to go but farther away. It was just survival, a ragged line between one place and the next, and a simple case of too many problems and not enough answers.

After the *Tanquetazo,* Santiago and the rest of the country quieted down ever so slightly, if only to lick its wounds and reload. The protests continued and rumors of new coup attempts circulated on a daily basis. Both sides were arming and deploying their paramilitaries, but it was clear to me that the military would win this arms race. No matter how committed they were, a devoted band of union workers was no match for a treasonous Chilean Army.

On July 17, *Patria y Libertad* founder Roberto Thieme declared that the militia would unleash an armed offensive to overthrow the government. As for the UP partisans, the Movement of the Revolutionary Left was building arms caches and training. Each side was slowly but surely preparing for the next phase of battle.

On July 27, Sergeant Arturo Araya Peeters was assassinated by a sniper's bullet outside of his front door. Peeters was a close Allende ally and one of the last high-ranking members left in the military that opposed military intervention. Thirty-two members of *Patria y Libertad* were detained for questioning about the murder, including JC's boss. All but one were released after pressure was brought to bear on the prosecuting attorneys. After initially fleeing the country, one co-conspirator was sentenced to three years in prison. A man named Augusto Pinochet would later pardon the murderer.

I never understood how JC could work for *Patria y Libertad,* even indirectly. The political assassinations, the deceit, the fascist ultimatums for obedience—there was enough self-righteous malice in that one militia to take down the entire country. They had even taken out a full-page ad in the newspaper claiming responsibility for the *Tanquetazo.* How could he look in the mirror and not feel ashamed? I could only reason that hate had overtaken him. Anyone can find a reason to hate, if they look hard enough. For some of us, we don't have to look very hard.

The blood streaming down his face failed to mask the ragged laceration on his cheek.

"What the hell happened?"

"Fucking *milicos*," Cody growled through clenched teeth.

The other knife wound, a jagged incision stretching from his elbow to his bicep, was only visible after he took off his bloodied coat.

"Are you all right?" I compressed the arm wound with a towel but Cody continued to lose blood.

"Yeah, I'll be fine. It's not that bad."

"Fuck you, it's not that bad. You're bleeding like a stuck pig." I tied another towel around the wound.

"Goddamnit Cody, what happened this time? Where were you?"

Cody looked around the room for an escape route but JC and I had him surrounded.

"I was at a friend's house and some soldiers raided the place. I was the only one to get away."

"Jesus, Cody. What were you doing at a house that was raided by soldiers?"

JC interrupted. "You were buying drugs. Right? And they were there to bust you?"

Cody ignored the question. "I fought my way out of the apartment. One soldier tracked me to the back alleyway but I waited for him in the back alley and choked him out."

"Did anyone see you come back here?" I asked.

"I'm pretty sure no one saw me."

"Pretty sure?" JC asked, incredulous. "If you're wrong, they're going to hunt us down."

JC was right and we all knew it. If they had seen Cody enter the building they would raid every single apartment looking for him.

"No one saw me. Calm the fuck down."

"Cody, I'm sick of your bullshit," JC said. "We brought you here to help you, and you've only become more of a junkie. You're a lost cause."

JC stormed out of the apartment, stopping only to punch a hole in the wall.

Shame spread over Cody's face. "I admit it. I need heroin. But at least I'm still alive."

I helped him walk over to the sink to clean the wound. As I re-wrapped his arm with the towel I realized that Cody was right about one thing. He was still better off than the men who never made it out. No matter how bad it got, at least he had survived.

After helping Cody bandage his wounds (and foolishly giving him a glass of whisky to dull the pain) I went to the bakery to walk Ayelen home. She felt safer walking at night when I was with her. I kissed her goodnight and promised I would see her soon.

When I returned to the apartment, Cody was sitting slumped in a chair like a folded ragdoll. Ever the trusty sidekick, the near-empty bottle of whisky rested predictably at his side.

"Really? You're drunk again? Good for you."

"It doesn't matter," he replied. "When can we go back to California?"

"Man, I don't know. We deserted the Army—they're not waiting for us with open arms. If we go back, we'll go to prison for a long time."

"How long? I can't be here anymore. If I don't go now I'm never going to make it back."

"You could handle being behind bars again? I'll lose my mind if someone puts me back in a cell."

"So would I," he said. "But things aren't working out so well here, are they?"

Neither of us knew what would happen if we returned, and short of sitting through a court martial there was no easy way to find out. There was one thing we *did* know about desertion, though, something that the Army had gone to great lengths to communicate: the death penalty was on the table. Although Cambodia was never far from our minds, the possibility of going to prison had emerged as an all too probable best-case scenario, one only slightly better than an Army firing line. That is, unless we stayed in Chile the rest of our lives.

Cody hadn't seen a sunrise in months but he was up at the crack of dawn the next morning, nursing a cup of coffee and squinting through bleary hangover eyes. I imagined he had spent the night like me, wide awake with a spinning-top mind, mulling over bad options like unpaid bills in the hope they might resolve themselves. We had agreed to go to the library to research how long we might spend in a Fort Leavenworth cell if we surrendered to Uncle Sam.

As we walked to the library on Avenida Providencia, skinny rays of sun pierced through the morning haze lording over Santiago. The library's front portico was a tangle of overhanging shadows bending around marble columns, and the shadows only intensified inside the library. The wood-paneled room was empty save a prim librarian stacking books, and the leathery thuds echoed through the cavernous library. We weaved between metal shelves searching for books about American military law. After half an hour of searching the shelves, Cody found a yellowed copy of the United States Uniform Code of Military Justice.

The manual, though, was of little use. We learned only that we *were* in fact eligible for the death penalty because we had deserted in time of war. While it seemed unlikely that the Army would execute us, we had no idea how they were treating deserters, especially Special Forces troopers that had abandoned one of the most decorated units in the Army and fled to a Communist country.

Outside, the morning air was crisp and the gray sky was beginning to bleed blue. Across the street, voices emanated from the front steps of a mighty Catholic church adorned by Ionic columns that reached up to the steeple like exalting arms. The church bells rang and men in suits and women in dresses poured outside onto the street, awaiting a newly married couple. Little girls angled for position to see the couple before they disappeared into the waiting limo. When the bride and groom appeared on the front steps, the girls squealed and threw rice at the beaming newlyweds.

Then I noticed Cody, watching even more intently than I had been. He was so entranced by the wedding that he didn't hear my question, even though I was standing right next to him.

"Do you want to leave yet? This has been depressing."

"No, I want to see this. Let's stick around a few minutes."

Cody turned back to the wedding just as the newlyweds' car drove away, his gaze fixed on the guests hugging and parting ways in the street. We stood and looked on as the crowd dispersed and walked to their cars.

"All right, we can go."

On the walk back to the apartment, Cody stopped and turned to me.

"Even after everything that's happened, and we're criminals back home—we can still get married, right?"

"Of course, Cody. Of course."

We finished the walk home in silence.

When I thought back on what he said I was startled by his innocence, asking the most childish of questions. I realized how young he was, and how young I was, and how much time we still had left. And then I didn't feel so old anymore.

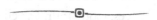

The few possessions that traveled with us crossed the ocean not once but twice, stowaway cargo hauled to the ends of the earth and back: A silver crucifix with the Savior wrapped around the cross like an ivy vine. A sea lion made of tiny black and gray conch shells, a gift from my parents. An ivory button. JC carried an Argentinean peso Father gave him when we crossed the border and drove through the ghostly pampas.

These were our mementos, weary baubles with reservoirs of goodwill that were drained a long time ago, somewhere on the banks of the Mekong or in the incinerated foothills of central Vietnam. After each ocean passage they came to seem more like artifacts from an ancient civilization than things from our past, memories pilfered by runaways to claim a history that wasn't really their own. Why else carry a cracked ivory button from a mother's white dress? I knew why, but it was hard to believe that these salvaged items represented full chapters of our lives. I kept the artifacts in a red tobacco tin my father had used when we were children. The tin sat next to my bed, close enough to reach. I just wanted to know that those things, and the times they came from, were still real.

One day, when the loss of our old life hurt more than usual, I was sorting through the tin's contents, trying to remember each item's origin.

"It's strange, isn't it?" Cody said when he saw me looking at the items. "The things that survive along with you."

"What do you mean?"

"When I think about the few possession that have made it this far, I can't help but ask what they're doing in Chile. It just seems surreal, you know?"

"Not really."

"To me, it's hard to believe that a magnet my mom bought me in 5th grade is in Santiago, Chile right now, in the ratty apartment where I live. And that a few months before it was packed away in an Army backpack being lugged through the Cambodian bush. And that I'm a fugitive here, and there. It seems too strange to be real."

JC walked in while Cody was talking.

"What are you talking about, Cody? Are you high again?"

"Not sure you would understand. It's kind of philosophical."

JC stared at him dryly. "Try me."

Cody had learned how to deflect JC's anger in his own way. Instead of confronting it head on like me, he managed to laugh it off, pissing JC off in the process.

"I was saying that our lives have become too unreal to believe that they're real."

"What does that even mean, Cody? The words you're saying, they don't make any sense."

"Once upon a time there was a life in California where the hours of the day made sense. There was a rhyme and a reason to the day, a reason why I woke up in the morning, went to school, went to football practice. That life made sense."

"And now," he continued, "the fact that me and my Purple Heart and my magnet are in Chile don't make any sense. They make this moment a lot harder to accept as reality."

JC was flummoxed. "What you're saying still doesn't make any sense. Of course you are here right now. Where else would you be? What else would be your *reality*?" The word was issued with a thick layer of condescension.

They scowled at each other. Cody was annoyed with JC for failing to understand his point, and slightly bemused. JC, on the other hand, was *infuriated* with Cody for not understanding why he was being so absurd. How would JC ever be able to understand Cody's babbling? It was absurd to presume that something so irrational could ever make any sense.

I knew what Cody was trying to say, that what our lives had become did not make sense because they had turned out so wrong. And that being holed up in a shabby apartment hiding from the Chilean *and* American armies was so comically backward as to be inconceivable. Things were so bad that they just couldn't be real.

And I knew what JC was trying to say, that of course we are here and of course this is our reality, just like sleeping in rainwater and interrogating villagers and attacking Cambodian barges was our reality, just like fleeing Chile because Father was a CIA spy was our reality.

And losing our angel mother to a bullet meant for someone else was reality.

I knew what they both meant, and I knew they would never understand each other, and I knew there was nothing I could do about it.

I sat between my bitter twin brother and my heroin-addict best friend and listened to the sound of deafening anger.

That night I dreamed of the past. It was spring and we were playing in the backyard. The jacarandas were in full bloom and the violet petals formed a brilliant corona around the house. The sky was clear despite the pattering rain, and sunlight streamed through the raindrops and reflected off the dewy petals. We had both gotten sunburned at the beach earlier that day and my cheeks were warm in the cool rain.

"You can't catch me," JC squealed as we sprinted through the yard, raindrops pelting our skinny bare chests. I stuck my tongue out as I ran to catch the fat drops of honey rain falling from the translucent sky. JC was ahead of me, his thick mop of hair bouncing around his freckled face, running with his arms spread like an airplane and howling deliriously happy little-boy yelps. He looked like he could run on top of those big fat raindrops, like a staircase, all the way to heaven.

Then, right then, was the best moment of my life. I have never felt like that since. But why?

Then I remembered something else.

She was standing on the steps wearing her favorite white dress with ivory buttons, her wavy dark curls sparkling in the rain as she watched over us. Our mother. The sun and moon and stars of our safe and sunburned little-boy world.

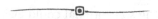

Because Ayelen's parents didn't know about us, the only way I could talk to her was by going to the bakery where she worked. I would knock at the window and one of the girls would scamper back to the ovens to tell her I was outside. One Sunday, though, a coworker came back and told me she couldn't see me. I returned every morning for the next four days, and each day they told me the same thing. On Friday morning I burst into the bakery, desperate for an explanation.

"Where is Ayelen?"

"She's in back—but she can't see you right now. She's busy." The girl who spoke was the same one who had couriered messages for us before.

"I need to see her." I was frantic, on the verge of losing control.

Ayelen walked out of the back room, pulling off a white apron. She was covered by a white mist of flour.

"I'm sorry, everybody. I'll be back in a few minutes." Without saying another word she gestured for me to follow her through the kitchen and out the back door.

"Why won't you talk to me? What did I do?" I said.

"Please don't yell at me. I was going to talk to you soon."

"Talk about what? What's going on?"

"*Mi amor*, I don't know what to do. My mother found out I didn't come to work the nights I was with you."

"So we'll come up with something. We'll figure it out."

"But she demanded to know where I was. I had to tell her that I was with you."

Ayelen was crying softly. "She says I need to stop seeing you or she'll tell Father. I'm scared that he'll beat us both."

"I'm not going to lose you because of him. He won't hurt either of you—I'll make him understand what I will do to protect you."

"But he'll kick me out, too. Where will I go?" Fear splintered her words.

I put my hands on her shoulders and looked in her eyes. Later, she would tell me that I had *ojos locos,* crazy eyes that both loved and scared her.

"We can go to Patagonia. Ever since I came back I've wanted to ask you to move there. Come with me."

"But where would we live?"

"Land is cheap, and I have enough money to buy a small plot. We can build a house. I promise I'll take care of you."

"Benjamin, I don't think I can leave my family. They're all I have."

"I lost my family a long time ago, and I've had to rebuild one from the pieces that were left. But we can do it together. You'll have a family again, the kind you deserve."

"What about my mother?"

"If she wants, she can come with us. We'll be safe and we won't have to run away anymore. Please come with me. I love you."

She put her hand on my cheek and searched my eyes for a reason to trust. She must have found one.

"All right. Yes. I'll go with you."

With that, a love-struck boy and a dancing girl with a lightning bug smile chose their fates. Pending approval of the outside world.

The day was foggy, with soft edges. We had come to Valparaiso to see Father. After learning that we were in Chile he decided to come see us, at long last. We were meeting at the beach our family used to visit when we were kids. JC and I walked along the coastline looking for his familiar jowly face. We came upon a soccer game that stretched the width of the beach, with one end of the field just shy of the rolling waves. Men of all ages were flowing back and forth between goals made of sticks planted upright in the sand. We waited until the play moved to the other end of the beach and jogged across the field.

Father stood at the crest of the beach where the waves were breaking. He seemed taller than I remembered, his shoulders confidently upright and his back ramrod straight. There was a purpose in the way he carried himself that I hadn't seen since before we fled Chile. Next to him stood a beautiful woman with long dark hair. She was wearing a flowing white dress. Father had his arm around the woman's waist. They stood unmoving, looking out over the ocean as the waves rolled over their bare feet. JC and I called out from the distance.

"*Papá*! *Papá*! We're over here!" We shouted at the top of our lungs but our voices were muffled by the winds blowing in from the restive ocean.

There was a commotion from inland. A group of young men were arguing and pushing each other, and heading directly at us. A fight was breaking out.

One man yelled *Marxistas culiados* and threw a vicious right hook that caught his target on the chin. The recipient of the punch crumpled to the ground and two other attackers began kicking and stomping him. More fighters joined the clash, attacking each other with wild punches and kicks. An older man fell and attempted to cover his bleeding face, but the assailants pulled back his arms to continue the beating. We couldn't tell if there were sides—everyone seemed to be fighting everyone else.

JC and I rushed into the fray to try to stop the battle, to no avail. A huge man with a thick black beard took a swing at JC before melding back into the riotous mass. I lost sight of Father through the swirl of clashing bodies.

The fighting finally started to move toward shore, although several men were left prostrate and bloodied on the ground. In the distance, we saw Father in the same place, staring at the ocean.

"*Papá*! Are you all right? Are you hurt?" I yelled as we ran up behind him.

"I'm fine, boys." He turned his gaze down the beach.

"Where did that woman go? Who was she?" JC asked.

"It doesn't matter. She's gone."

As he spoke, the sound of the brawl neared once again.

"But you obviously knew her. Who was she?"

"Trust me, it doesn't matter. She's gone."

As he spoke I heard a whooshing sound, and then a powerful blow crushed the back of my head.

I woke up in my bed, sweating profusely, with a deep-down ache in my chest. My dreams had also turned to the past, to losses borne by all that could never be shared and would never go away.

After Ayelen agreed to come with me, I could think of little else other than our new life together. The circumstances weren't what I had envisioned, but it was a new start. I vowed to bring everyone, if they would come. I vowed to fulfill my promise to Cody.

That morning was a regular workday, a chilly Tuesday in early spring. I finished my night shift. Walking outside after the shift, the streets around *La Voz del Pueblo* were mayhem. People were running in every direction, panic scrawled across their faces. Car horns were blaring through columns of clogged traffic.

Then I heard the unmistakable sound of artillery radiating from downtown.

A newspaper vendor was shouting from behind a kiosk but his voice was drowned out by the disorder of the street. I pushed through the crowd and neared the older man. His face was drained of color, his eyes as wide as saucers. I had seen those eyes before. I had seen that fear before.

The army is attacking La Moneda! The army is attacking La Moneda!

On the morning of September 11, in the year of our Lord 1973, a military junta led by the Commander of the Army Augusto Pinochet, General of the Air Force Gustavo Leigh, Navy Admiral José Toribio Merino, and General César Mendoza of the national police, launched a coup d'état against the democratically elected Chilean government. General Leigh, incidentally, was the man I had met as a boy in my father's office, the menacing Air Force officer with the black mole.

Upon learning of the coup, President Allende went directly to La Moneda with his bodyguards. At first he didn't believe that Pinochet was part of the *Golpe*, mistakenly believing that the Junta must have kidnapped the man he had only recently appointed Commander in Chief. It wasn't until later that he learned that Pinochet was a leader in the military putsch.

After bombing radio stations all over Santiago and raiding political headquarters, unions and homes of UP sympathizers, the military threatened to bomb La Moneda unless Allende resigned and surrendered. Allende refused to resign his office. Shortly thereafter, firefights broke out between the military and Allende's personal bodyguard unit, and armored tanks shelled the palace. Hawker Hunter jets followed up the ground assault by dropping missiles on the presidential grounds. By mid-afternoon the Allende loyalists that survived had surrendered to the Junta. Many others had already been killed in the attacks.

Shortly before the military stormed his office in La Moneda, Allende gave a farewell speech on Radio Magallanes.

I heard only the last part of the speech, but I carried the words with me.

Long live Chile! Long live the people! Long live the workers! These are my last words, and I am certain that my sacrifice will not be in vain....

Hearing those words, the anger boiled up in me. At the military for their betrayal, at Allende for believing his martyrdom to be grander than all the others, and at all of them for marching Chile to war. Yet I couldn't help but marvel at his certainty. While I wanted to believe that those who were sacrificed died for a noble cause, I was less certain of the reason so many were taken.

Allende died moments after giving the speech, reportedly by his own hand, though this point has been disputed. What is certain is that he was the victim of a bullet whose provenance will remain a mystery.

My mother was the victim of just such a bullet, one with no origin and no blame.

I heard Allende's speech over the radio as I was running to Ayelen's house. The moment the shelling started—the moment I saw the old man's panic-stricken face, the same fear that I had seen on so many grunts' faces when they first realized that they could die, might die, probably would die—my mind slipped back to the war. Back to the jungle, to the incoming terror of shrieking mortars and the mangled remains of those unlucky enough to be underneath. Among all the people that I needed to save, Ayelen came first. The only thing left to do was to find her and leave Santiago before our fragile new world crumbled.

Está norteando, I realized.

Wishing today was not today, and tomorrow was not tomorrow.

Está norteando.

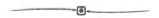

Ayelen was gone. The military had raided her home looking for her father, undoubtedly because of his position as a union head. In the apartment there were three bloodstains on the carpet, dark thin trails that ran solemnly from the corner of the room to the open door. Ayelen's neighbor, a frail elderly woman who lived next door, cried when I told her I was Ayelen's boyfriend. She said she heard the soldiers break down the door, then shouting, and then the pop-pop-pop of three gun shots.

All was quiet except for the whistle of the wind that weaved through the open doors and windows of homes and lives that halted abruptly, mid-sentence, when the soldiers came. With no time to say goodbye.

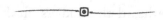

Suyai and Salvador were gone. Their street was decimated, a silent witness to a brutality whose only traces were broken-down doors, scattered clothes, tire tracks and bullet holes. Their home was empty and had been ransacked. The portrait of Cristián that had hung on the far bedroom wall had been torn down and ripped into pieces. The stove was left on, and a small fire burned under the grill. A cold pot of bean soup sat undisturbed on the table. The only trace of either of them was Salvador's ball in the front hallway. If Suyai had been there she would have gently scolded him, for the millionth time, to keep the ball outside. In its place, the wind whistled through the hallway and out the shattered backdoor.

I heard footsteps behind me. I turned and saw Jorge running up to the house.

"You've got to get out of here," he said. His trucker's uniform was stained red and there was a gash on his forehead caked with dry blood.

"Where are Suyai and Salvador?"

"They were taken away by the Army. They came looking for her as soon as they entered the barrio."

"What do we do now?"

"Right now, just try to stay alive. I'll keep working to get more information about them. Where are Cody and JC?"

"I don't know. Cody was going to meet me at the newspaper. I don't know where JC is."

"Go and get Cody. You're all in danger right now, because they'll know that you know Suyai and me. But you're still Americans—if we can get you to the U.S. Embassy you'll be safe. Meet me back here tonight at ten o'clock."

"I'll try," I said as Jorge ran out the door.

I arrived back at *La Voz del Pueblo* to find that the office had been razed. Circular craters scooped out by exploding bombs bowed down into the ground like carelessly dug graves. The overhead lights were dangling precariously from electric cables that swung from the lobby ceiling. *La*

Voz del Pueblo had been the target of aircraft missiles, I knew, because I had seen American planes leave similar pockmarks in Vietnamese factories and hamlets. The front wall of the main newsroom had collapsed, leaving a pile of broken cement that blocked a view of the newsroom and Ricardo's office in the back. I called out but was met with silence.

Leaping over the collapsed wall, I saw the remains of the newsroom. Most of the desks had been demolished, and a small fire burned in the corner, slowly consuming whatever remained in its path. At the far end of the newsroom, through a cloud of sticky smoke, Ricardo's office was faintly visible. The corner columns had collapsed inward on the office. It resembled a campfire when the burning logs collapse upon themselves and turn to smoldering embers. I continued calling out for survivors but still no answer came. I zigzagged through the debris to Ricardo's office, beginning to hope that somehow all my colleagues had escaped.

Ricardo's arms were outstretched on top of the wide mahogany desk, newly blackened by the smoke. The telephone receiver lay overturned next to his editing pen, and the cigarette tray sat untouched on the far corner of the desk, full of spent cigarettes. A steel beam had fallen on top of the desk and partially blocked his face.

Moving around the side of the desk, I saw that the beam had landed on his chest. The blow had spared his face. Ash from the fire had settled in his bushy eyebrows, turning them from white to silvery black. I was alone in the office of the man who had known my secret and trusted me anyway.

"Stop!" It was a young man's voice coming from behind the pile of rubble. I turned and saw a uniformed soldier with his rifle pointed at me.

The Army soldier was no more than a boy. He wore a wispy imitation of a mustache on his upper lip, and his fatigues hung loosely off of a wire-thin frame. Outside of the building, more soldiers' voices echoed in the street, but he was the only one who had entered the crumbled wreckage of the newsroom.

"Stop!" he repeated, raising the rifle to his chest. "You're under arrest for breaking the curfew established by the Junta." He was more than thirty feet away from me, but even from that distance I could see that he was shaking.

I looked the boy in the eyes and pleaded mercy. "Please. I can't go with you. They'll kill me." He was slowly walking toward me with the rifle still raised.

"You have to understand," I said. "I just need to find my friend. Please, let me go. I haven't done anything wrong."

What would I have done if I were him? I would have done what I had done before. I would have fired, as I was trained to do.

Out of the corner of my eye I saw a flash of movement behind the young soldier, but he didn't see it. It looked like a civilian carrying a police baton.

"If you run I have to shoot you," the boy said. "If I don't, they will shoot me. You understand? It's you, or me."

Raising the rifle once again, he looked down the barrel and squared me in his sights.

It took no more than a second. JC ran out from behind a crumbled cement pillar, baton raised above his head.

"Run!" JC yelled as he clubbed the soldier over the head. The boy screamed as he fell to the ground. As JC again swung the club, I saw two more soldiers enter the front door with rifles raised, scanning the newsroom. They hadn't seen JC yet.

JC held the bloodied truncheon in his hand, and in between blows he looked up at me with pleading eyes.

"Go. Please. Save yourself." The last thing I saw was JC turning to face the two soldiers at the door.

As I ran out the backdoor I heard a volley of gunfire. Then, silence. The jet-black alleyway behind the newspaper stretched on forever.

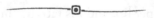

I don't remember anything about the trip back to the apartment other than running through empty streets and feeling a hurt too big to hold inside. JC standing in that firing line played and re-played in my mind's eye. My brother was dead.

Cody was the only person left. If I found him, we could still meet Jorge and get to the American Embassy. Maybe I could still get him out alive.

I approached the apartment through the back alleyway. Creeping up the rusting staircase, I passed the second floor and peeked around the corner to our apartment. The light bulb outside the door was shattered and the staircase was darkened by long shadows.

As I edged up the final flight of stairs I saw that the apartment door had been kicked down. I pulled out the butterfly knife I had carried since the *Tanquetazo*, flipped open the blade and gripped the handle tightly in my palm. Peering around the corner of the door, I saw that the kitchen was empty. With my back against the wall I moved toward the living room, sliding past the hole that JC had punched in anger.

The window had been left open. Sounds from the street filtered into our living room, furnished only by the torn couch and the small TV where Cody spent hours watching shows he couldn't understand. Even in the midst of that terrifying night, when families were hunkered down by radios awaiting the next ground-shaking announcement, the voices of children could be heard through open windows. Wondering what was to come next. Wondering if their families would be safe.

Cody lay on his back in the middle of the room. In his outstretched hand, a K-bar Army knife shimmered in the moonlight. Next to his head, a small crimson-colored pool of blood had stained the carpet and was marching outward, darkening the floor in cold, concentric circles. Cody's hand and the knife were bathed in blood. At least he died fighting.

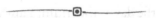

It was a day without the paper. Nothing extraordinary, a day without newspapers. Something we should all be able to live with. Something we should get over, with a little time.

There were no newspapers on September 12, 1973 because the Junta had yet to give permission for any Santiago daily—even those that had aided and abetted the *Golpe*—to go to print. For the few newspapers that survived the coup, the Junta required more time to edit and approve content. In some cases, military personnel were said to have personally written articles and were unable to meet print deadlines.

La Voz del Pueblo did not go to print that day. Its building was in ruins, destroyed by aircraft missiles, its editor-in-chief crushed by a dislodged steel beam. Ricardo had been reading copy when he was killed. The story in his hand was set to run the next day, an article reporting that many

Chileans still held out hope for a peaceful resolution to the constitutional crisis. The rest of the staff had fled for their lives, if they were still alive and not already under arrest.

As for other newspapers, they were bombed or stormed by the military, their printing presses destroyed or sitting unused. Many journalists unfortunate enough to have been at work that morning were taken prisoner. Many of them were later tortured, and some were killed, including an American journalist who was investigating the Schneider murder.

On September 12, the airwaves also went silent. Most radio stations had been commandeered by the Junta, and only approved decrees would be broadcast from that day forward. As for stations perceived to have sympathized with Allende, they were raided or destroyed. Radio Magallenes—the radio station that remained on air to broadcast Allende's farewell speech even after it was bombed by Air Force jets—was raided shortly after the speech, its journalists arrested and broadcast equipment razed by machine gun fire.

Only two Santiago dailies survived to print after September 11: *El Mercurio*, in all its insurrectionist glory, and a smaller daily called *La Tercera*. Both newspapers would soon offer monetary awards for turning in suspected *Unidad Popular* functionaries. Turning in these fellow Chileans for detainment, persecution and torture, the papers preached, was a citizen's duty. *El Mercurio* ruled the day as the triumphant voice in the once raucous debate over the future of Chile. A merciless prophet shouting the gospel truth at a pile of bodies.

After September 11, the Junta began to collect a cumbersome number of political prisoners. While some were killed during or after the *Golpe*, there were thousands of men and woman who were either known political operators or supporters of the Allende administration, or were suspected of being so. Requiring an unusually large space to detain these political prisoners, the Junta selected the Estadio Nacional, one of the only locations where thousands of prisoners could be held out of public sight. Out of sight, perhaps—but not out of earshot. Prisoners were often sent to the stadium. Many of them never returned.

To live close to the stadium after the *Golpe* was to hear the unvarnished sounds of human anguish. Suyai's neighbors later said that the worst part wasn't the screams that came from within the stadium's walls. Rather, it was the unnatural sounds—the crackles and snaps and strange bellows—that terrified anyone living near the improvised prison. It was said, later, that the Junta used Brazilian torture experts that hung prisoners from chains and sent electric pulses through their bodies, and that the torturers attached the steel alligator clips of the electric cables to prisoners' faces, nipples and genitalia. It was said, later, that soldiers refusing to follow orders to torture or execute prisoners were themselves shot, turning young boys into freshly minted killers, or the *Golpe's* latest victims. It was said, later, that a man called *El Encapuchado—the Hooded One*—roamed the stadium with a brown paper bag over his head, peering through two crudely cut eye holes and indiscriminately executing prisoners. Suyai's neighbors said, later, that they were stalked by the nightly cries of female prisoners pleading *Please No, Please No* to impervious attackers, crying out to a world unable or unwilling to help.

I never found out how Suyai was detained. After discovering her unpacking rifles that night I learned that she and Jorge had been smuggling munitions in from Argentina for months. Having served as a Special Forces soldier in the United States Army, I was in the unique but dispiriting position of understanding the futility of their endeavor. These people would die fighting against a much more powerful enemy. But I couldn't bring myself to tell them that a handful of rusty AK-47s wouldn't save them any more than they had saved a nation of Vietnamese peasants that chose the wrong government.

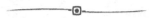

The next day Jorge dropped me off in front of the American Embassy.

"Son, you have to go. There's nothing here left for you. I'll write with news about Suyai and Salvador if I learn anything. I'm sorry. For Ayelen—for everything."

"But what's left for me now?"

"I don't know. Live. And pray for us."

When I reached the gate outside the Embassy I was met by Army soldiers with rifles crossed imperially across their chests. I raised my hands above my head and yelled to the nearest soldier as I approached the gate.

"Don't shoot. I'm an American citizen. I'm a soldier in the US Army."

The teenage grunt raised an eyebrow and then consulted with an older officer before opening the gate. As the soldier checked my documents and patted me down, I heard a clamor behind me as Chileans trying to enter were turned away. But I didn't look back. Shame kept my eyes fixed straight ahead as they led me through the Embassy's marble columns. I couldn't bear to look back at those left behind.

When the Army plane—a Hercules C-130 cargo transport, ironically—lifted off the runway that bitter night of September 12, 1973 and left Santiago behind, I traced the silhouette of the Andes through the window and wondered when I would see its shrouded skyline again.

Praying it would be my last escape, I promised I wouldn't lead anyone else into harm's way. But even then I knew it would be a hard promise to keep. Who can foresee the dangers ahead? I, for one, had already failed with grave results. So what was left was to keep everyone at a safe distance.

How do you live with the things you've done, and face up to the burden of years stolen and lives destroyed? You can't. Not really, and if you try to make sense of it, a haunting madness begins to creep in. So you try to forget, even though you know it's impossible.

PART V

SHELL BEACH, CALIFORNIA: PRESENT DAY

Our house is a shrine to the children's lives and accomplishments, from the stellar to the categorically run-of-the-mill. Hope has been meticulous about procuring and saving these artifacts: the trophies, ribbons and certificates of achievement (and participation); art projects, Christmas ornaments and stick-figured crayon drawings from darling but artistically challenged children. They are everywhere, pleasant reminders of the life Hope and I have built in this California refuge.

The mantel is lined with their pictures in various stages of adolescence, photos assembled in tidy little ovals with a glossy 90's sheen that dates their childhoods and the wondrously maddening years we spent raising them. The photos begin with the adorable early years, round through the awkward pubescent ones and then neatly conclude with a photo of an adult, a grown person replete with rapidly forming habits and hopes and mysteries.

There's Thomas, with a look of older-brother seriousness mocked only ever so slightly by the oversized blazer draped over his lean teenage shoulders; Nathan, hair mussed and smiling mischievously, barely able to contain his amusement at a joke that only he seems to get; and Maribel, my dear Maribel, so calm and composed and beautiful. When I stop to look at these markers of time I am eternally grateful for those years, but I can't help but feel a little confused, too. I can't help but wonder why I wasn't able to save anything from other periods of my life. I don't have a single keepsake from Ayelen, or my aunt or my brother, either. How can you go through life and collect a surplus of memories, and nothing else?

Packed away somewhere is the one thing that I managed to keep. I still question whether I had the right to keep it in the first place, but I did. Selfishly, perhaps, but Cody's death was my loss, too. In the last three years of his life, when all he got from his parents were form letters praising his patriotism and saying little else, and when JC lost patience with Cody the junkie and forgot Cody the friend and brother-in-arms—in those last years, I was the closest person to him in the world. I reasoned that I deserved something for that, and that the mark we left on each other's lives was at the very least worth something to remember him by. At the very least.

When I found Cody in the apartment after the *Golpe*, I bent down to say goodbye. As I gently closed his eyes I saw the St. Christopher pendant hanging around his neck. I thought back to him rubbing the silver pendant and praying as we left Valparaiso, and of conceding our dog tags before the Cambodia missions, and of the men who died there who weren't allowed to carry anything to pass on. I carefully unclipped the chain's clasp that rested on his collar and took with me the only thing I could.

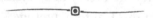

My mother was an insatiable reader, not only of the Good Book but of classics and poetry and anything else with pages bound between covers. On the wall of her study—really just a cove in the attic with a desk and a small shelf where she kept her books—there was a poem that hung on the wall. There were only a dozen or so stanzas on the weathered page, but she had underlined one in particular:

> *Me rebelo a morir, pero es preciso...*
> *¡El triste vive y el dichoso muere!...*
> *¡Cuando quise morir, Dios no lo quiso,*
> *Hoy que quiero vivir, Dios no lo quiere!*

I asked her on several occasions what those strange, beautiful lines meant—*I rebel against death, but it's precise/The sad live and the happy die*—but her answer was always the same, as if prepared for an oral exam by rote memorization.

It's just a sad poem, mi amor. Sometimes beautiful things are sad.

It was like her answer to our questioning of which of us she loved more. *I love you both with all my heart,* she would say, the answer as dependable as our nightly bedtime stories. Even at that age the fractions didn't add up and we clamored to claim our rightful share of our mom's love, but it was the only answer she ever gave. *Both of you. With all my heart.*

Wanting something does not make it so. Most of what we learned as children was from our Mom, but that was one of the few lessons we learned from Father. He never articulated it, or even realized he was teaching it, but he didn't need to. We witnessed the slow but certain undoing of a man who wanted his wife back more than he wanted his leftover life without her. But he could not will it so. And he wanted to blame someone so badly that he struck out with blind fury at a fictitious enemy. The most impressionable lessons, it seems, are the ones that don't need to be taught at all.

Parents try to teach based on the lives they lived, but there is only so much of any life that can be pried open and shared. My mother's life was like that, a kindhearted country girl who married a hard-to-love man but loved him anyway for the sake of her family. There is a limit to how much can be taught, but what can be learned is infinite.

I understood later why she didn't explain the poem to me. There are some hard truths from which children should be spared. But as much as she wanted to shelter us from certain truths, she couldn't. And as much as I want to silence the midnight skeletons, I can't. And as much as revisiting the past won't change anything, I'll still try.

Years ago, when the kids were in various stages of adolescence and Hope and I were busier than ever running the business and shuttling the kids around, Hope's father became sick. He was a private man, securely Midwestern in his sensibilities, and he never explained what was happening to his body. He just let Hope know that his time was short and that we should come to visit him soon. Hope told me he often said that he was tired, just bone tired.

In those months, while his body wasted away and his mind started to go with it, Hope became very quiet. It was more than just sadness, though that was part of it. She wore a look of deep concentration, like her mind was somewhere far away.

We made it back to Michigan and saw him before he died, and even when his body failed and his mind faded there were moments of comfort with his family. He had lived the right way, as a good husband and father. Hope spoke at the funeral, uncommon for a daughter, but she was always her daddy's little girl and she loved him accordingly. On the plane ride home I asked her what had brought on the quietness those past months.

"I was thinking about what to say about him. He was a good man, you know? Not rich or famous, but a noble man all the same. I owed it to him to tell his story the right way, so that people remembered him as he was."

There are many reasons why I love my wife, but her goodness comes above all else. She was right. It was a life. They all deserve to be remembered, even the ordinary ones. Especially the ordinary ones.

There's a sacred connection forged in the last hours of life that binds survivors to the departed. In those final moments, time stands still. Codas are written, promises are made and sins are forgiven. Every second of dying pulsates with life, with illumination and the presence of the divine. But after witnessing this sacred ritual and coming face to face with the mystery of death, we must return to regular lives. To the mundane, the ordinary and the agnostic; to deadlines, bills and doctor's appointments. And then, without ever wanting to, we begin to forget.

I try to remember my mother every day, but sometimes it's like I tried too hard to hold on to the best memories and they slipped away through my too-tightly clenched fists. It hurts more than never having remembered in the first place. It is losing a part of you, and then losing it anew.

I have forgotten what she said to JC and me when we came inside that afternoon so many springs ago, after she watched us from the porch in her white dress while we sprinted through the rain under a halo of brilliant jacaranda petals. I know she tousled our wet hair as we came through the back door and wrapped big towels around our skinny bodies, and I know she spoke soothing words as she led us upstairs to change clothes. I know all this because I knew her then better than I knew myself.

I know what she would have said as she wrapped the fresh white towels around us and gave us wide-wrapping hugs. *You boys are crazy*, her gentle laugh levitating in the air. *Let's get you into some warm clothes.*

But I can no longer hear her or see her speaking those words. No matter how deeply I burrow down to find that memory I come up empty. Forgetting her is the greatest lament of my life, and I can't undo it. We all forget, and we become someone else, no matter how tenaciously we fight to hold on to the past.

I have a friend in San Luis Obispo that works as a homicide detective, John Taylor. John is kind of a gringo version of me, fat and balding, with the jowls and eye bags of a barroom regular. He was my first friend after I returned to California in September of 1973, because he was comfortable with drinking in silence and he didn't consider my melancholy as a personal affront. I just wanted to be left alone, and he obliged.

John's been on the force for nearly forty years but he refuses to retire. I think there are a few reasons why he keeps working. Like me, he's worried he'll drive his wife crazy if he's stomping around the house all day, and vice versa. But more importantly, John says that he doesn't want to lose the thing he's proudest of in life.

Being a cop is often thankless work. It turns out that writing traffic tickets and pulling over drunks can piss off neighbors just as often as it protects them. The pay isn't exactly stellar, either, especially for somebody trying to live on the gilded left coast. As for being a homicide detective, it's even harder, because it's your responsibility to bring some small measure of justice to families who have lost everything. You can never do enough, but you can definitely do too little. It's hard work, protecting others, and it can go wrong all too easily.

I've asked him if it's hard to deal with it all, the coroners' offices and cadavers and autopsies. John says that it's just part of the job. Given my own experience, I can't believe that investigating murders year after year doesn't take its toll. Yet he insists that it's not the bodies that trouble him.

"I can deal with seeing a victim," he said, "because I've come to believe that once the soul leaves the body, it's no longer the person. It's back to ashes and dust."

"But death isn't just the bodies," he added. "It's the silences when you can't help but ask how another person could do such a thing—could steal someone else's *life*. There's just no good answer."

When he told me that, I couldn't help but ask what had kept him going all those years.

"We've all got to pay the piper, Benjamin. All of us."

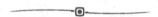

The first time we left Chile was in 1970, fleeing from the Communists and escaping to California. The second time was in 1973, running from Pinochet and the Junta. Chile underwent a sea change in those three years, swinging wildly from one extreme to the other. Nothing stayed the same and nothing was stable except the unrelenting instability, and the fact that no matter who was in charge we clearly were not welcome. Politics would bog down in a stalemate between extremists, ideologues seizing power and dismantling the country in order to rebuild it the *right way*. Society would be hopelessly divided, antiquated notions of class inflaming old grudges and new hatreds alike. And the Chilean people would condemn the violence while preemptively striking out against perceived enemies. Chile was a complicated place, a land of kind and generous people whose differences drove them to hate each other.

To have erred so gravely by transplanting us to Chile, based only on fear and blind optimism, remains hard to accept. What makes it harder is the realization that there was no better option. To this day I don't know what else we could have done. This singular thought has robbed me of countless nights of sleep, this trying to figure out how one responds when there is no good option. The injustice of being left without choice is staggering, and can break a man's spirit. But those bouts of self-pity don't last too long. They last only until I remember the millions of Vietnamese, and Chileans, and people all over the world who face that reality every day of their lives.

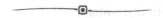

After fleeing to California for the second time, I moved into a cheap apartment near the coast and awaited military trial. But with thousands of young men returning to the States after dodging the draft, the government wasn't too concerned with prosecuting grunts—they were more worried about the felon in the White House. Even a sordid one-room tenement with chipped turquoise paint that smelled of turpentine and stale sex trumped living with my father. Despite the loss of everyone except the two of us, nary a word was offered in solace. Too much had been given, and too much had been taken. The prodigal son returned to a father who wasn't interested.

I often recalled something Mom used to say to Father when he became angry with his own family. *They are blood. For that reason alone you forgive them.* But I couldn't take her advice. The best I could muster was to act as if he didn't exist, which was better than battling and hating the old man. He died years later, an irascible old drunk accompanied only by his bottles and his bitterness.

In California the second time around, America was still fighting the Cold War, and I had plenty of time to ruminate on the wisdom of my homeland's flirtation with socialism. I was never a proponent of Communism or any of its variations, and I never will be. It seems that even a cursory knowledge of its historical failures would foster an apprehension of a world run by masters planning our lives and daily labor. But I've long since forsaken any *ism*, and am wary of any man ready to impose his ultimate truth on others. That was the real tragedy of the *Golpe*, that men used weapons and fear to tell other men how to live, and then punished those who didn't comply. And I fear that was the real tragedy of Vietnam. That, and all the lives that were taken.

I know only that I was led into a war as a young man, and I fought. In doing so I took the lives of others. Some of those that I killed were innocent. Perhaps I was innocent, too. Of this last point I am less sure. My brother, my best friend and I fled that battle and ran straight into the jaws of one more subplot in the same decadent global struggle, one laughably removed from our volition. It was there that I lost them both.

From the frayed pages of the Bible my mom gave me on my fifth birthday, I read and re-read Jeremiah 11:19:

> *"But I was like a gentle lamb that is led to the slaughter; and*
> *I knew not that they had devised devices against me...."*

There is much I do not know, but of this I am sure: Judgment rests not only in what we have done but on what we have refrained from doing. This life aches for justice, calls out for it in tortured tones, and relents only when the truth can stand firm and unadulterated in the annals of history. When we all stand and answer for our time.

It has been said that the moral arc of the universe is long, but bends toward justice. Or something to that effect, I don't remember exactly—my memory seems to get worse with every passing day. It seems all those years of purging history have rendered me unable to recall much at all. Either way, I commend anyone who believes it. And I hope they're right.

I am left to wonder if they would still be alive if I had done something different. When I am alone, and something reignites my ancient shoulder wound, I make the sign of the cross (a gesture I no longer really understand) and conclude by touching my frayed shoulder and whispering *Holy Ghost*. Then I say their names: Suyai. Cody. JC. Ayelen.

Where exactly does this moral arc begin to inflect toward justice? When does it start to become fair?

I remember a very few things from the days following the coup. Those things I do remember revisit like lightning bolts, sudden flashes that shatter the very ground beneath me and then disappear as quickly as they came.

Those things that I do remember: I remember riding with Jorge through the granular darkness of early dawn on September 12, weaving through backstreets to evade the tanks and sickly green jeeps that manned checkpoints across the city; I remember arriving at the American Embassy and seeing a line of Chileans stretching around the block begging for political asylum, the kind my father received after Allende's election; I remember standing beneath the black wrought-iron gates outside the

Embassy that rose high in the air like gothic spires, faithfully guarded by a legion of Army grunts; I remember the dishonor that washed over me when I looked back at the desperate faces of those people, knowing that they wondered who this privileged son was, this Chilean who was welcomed so swiftly into the discriminating arms of safety; and I remember flying out of Santiago in that American cargo plane, past the golden Cordillera, and losing a part of myself that I've never recovered.

The rest, I've surely chosen to forget. But now, a lifetime later, as an old man with a capitalist paunch and a big home in the California hills, I am forcing myself to remember. To confront the ghosts from a time when I fled one battlefield for another. Vietnam was a special and vivid hell for its combatants, and even more so for its victims. Making it out alive didn't mean I walked away with a clean slate, though. We were all victims, and we were all guilty, though the penalties meted out were far from equal.

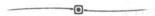

We'll never know exactly how many were sacrificed to undo Chile's socialist experiment. After a weary populace and *La Concertación* wrestled power from Pinochet, a slogging process began to document the atrocities committed by the Junta and its paramilitary appendages. The Valech Report produced an official number, I'm told. Despite the glaring missteps of the report— chief among them that some torture victims were forced to report abuses to officials that committed the original crimes, and that testimonies from younger victims were disregarded because they were irresponsibly unable to remember the details of torture they suffered in elementary school, or even kindergarten—I do appreciate the attempt to record the immensity of the abuse and loss of life. But for me, the report is woefully incomplete, to the point of being worthless. Those numbers don't bring back the only family I had left. And they certainly don't change what happened.

I hated Communism, then and now, for provoking dreams of smoke and lies and for making Chile a pawn in that dreaded game. I hated it because it bred an unworkable hope of a fair and egalitarian society, when humans are neither. And I hated it for turning that well-meaning wish into a graveyard, and for believing that others who stood to lose from its application would sit idly by. Men will fight, right or wrong, I should have known. We will fight, and we will die, even if we don't really understand why. And the few that give more than they take? They're the exception, not the rule.

Cody was the exception. A kind country boy from a broken home whose dad beat the hell out of him until the day he shipped off to Vietnam. A brave soldier who bore unspeakable pain to risk his life and sanity to save me. And a refugee who put his trust in a friend's promise, only to end up just like the rest of the GIs left behind in Southeast Asia, silent and unclaimed in a foreign land.

Suyai was the exception, giving everything for her family and her country until she had no more to give.

Ayelen was the exception, a princess with flying braids and a pure heart.

And my brother, my dear twin-faced brother, running with arms spread wide under a golden honey sky. Watching over and forgiving me for a future he would never see.

As the only one who survived, how dare I forget them? How dare I forget.

Four decades later, Chile was unrecognizable save for the Cordillera. The city's backdrop of white-capped peaks was now partitioned by self-important glass and steel structures, just one more sign of my old country's newfound affluence. Even the early 20ᵗʰ century government buildings, staid Georgian rectangles that lined the streets around La Moneda, looked stuffy and feeble next to shiny bank branches and corporate restaurants with slick focus-group tested names. Development, the long-coveted Holy Grail that to some justified the *Dictadura*, had finally arrived. Chile was an entirely different place, a bustling country with a brash economy and brimming confidence. As the country underwent this grand revival and the people became acquainted with the material comforts of rip-roaring capitalism, it was easy to see why Chileans were all too ready to leave those harrowing years behind.

Hope had decided to stay behind in California instead of joining my belated return to Chile. Thomas' wife was pregnant and needed help around the house, she said—a perfectly valid reason not to come and in keeping with Hope's selfless personality. But I sensed a deeper apprehension in her, a concern that by coming she might indulge and somehow prolong this fraught stroll down memory lane. Which was precisely what she *didn't* want to do. She wanted me back, or as much as she could get, and she wanted to put an end to the whiskey-fuelled fogs that wreaked havoc on our idyllic grandparent life. I didn't blame her, but I still had to come.

The trip to Chile was impromptu, an online purchase fueled by my recent bout of retrospection and more than a few tumblers. Taking the trip in May meant trading the sunny California summer for an ashen Santiago winter, but the thrill of year-round sun had lost its charm long ago. Leaving the business for a week was considerably harder, but Thomas has been feeling more comfortable running things all the time, and I'm trying to learn to trust his judgment in making the business' day-to-day decisions.

While it was hard to leave, I needed to get away. As much as that business has come to occupy the physical dimensions of my life—where I go and what I do seven days a week, fifty-two weeks a year—my mind checked out a long time ago. Nearly thirty-five years of hard work have put food on the table, a roof overhead and have paid for my kids' ludicrously expensive educations. Mission accomplished. To me, it has always been a means to an end. But what if you can never get to the end? Well, if you never get to the end, then the means is actually your end. There are quite simply better things to do in life.

The hotel in Santiago was located above a spacious Italian café with a burnished mahogany bar. Surveying the liquor selection, I saw several viable options, including a bottle of Dewar's sitting on a high shelf. I made a mental note to return if the trip took a turn for the worse. The hotel had smallish rooms with wood floors, blue shutters and flower print bedcovers that looked older than me. After arriving I tossed my suitcase on the bed and pried open the creaky French windows. The aroma of grilled steak drifted into the room from the street below. As I leaned over the balcony to get a glimpse of the barbecuing street vendors, I noticed a keyhole-sized view of Cerro Santa Lucia, the hill rising out of downtown Santiago that peers over the Bellas Artes neighborhood.

I found out from a young man working the front desk that there is now a *Museo de la Memoria*, a memorial to the victims of the dictatorship. The young man's family was monitored during the dictatorship, he told me, and the museum was an emotional experience for anyone who had lived through those years. He quickly added that even though his childhood was shaded by fear, he knew they were lucky to avoid the fate of the true victims of the terror, the exiled and tortured and the *desaparecidos*—the *disappeared*. I merely nodded, thanking him for the information, and forced myself to stay quiet as I felt the desperate potency of what I've been carrying inside all these years surge through my veins.

The day after I arrived I took a taxi to the museum, wondering what Chile's collective memory had retained.

The museum was modern and sleek, a glass and steel reminder that the human rights commissions are still recent history. After all, Chile needed fifteen years of democracy just to complete the Valech Report. The first floor of the museum features a length of plaques recognizing victims from thirty countries where dictatorships and human rights abuses led to imprisonment, torture and murder. Too many countries to list, too many militaries murdering their way to power. Chile truly was just one small piece of the puzzle.

The museum is home to many artifacts that one would expect from that era: bogus newspaper articles from *El Mercurio*, footage of soldiers raiding neighborhoods and beating prisoners, a recording of Pinochet ominously declaring that Chile would not return to democratic elections. I passed through the building slowly, trying to remember where I was when a particular speech or raid occurred. Then the decades raced away, and I remembered the fear and confusion and outrage as if it were happening all over again.

It was heartening to see footage of the *No* campaign, the public uprising before the '88 plebiscite that ended the dictatorship and returned Chile to democracy. The huge crowds in the streets faced down the Chilean military and marched bravely, defying the unspoken threats of violence from the past. The uncontrollable tears of older Chileans spoke volumes, but their joy was for future generations freed from the terror of dictatorial power. For older generations, the damage had already been done.

There were two things that I remember more than all the others. One was the letter—but that will come later.

The other was a collection of photographs that spanned the width and height of an entire museum wall, hundreds of feet tall and hundreds of feet wide. Thousands of small rectangular black and white photographs broken up by scattered blank white frames. A collage of the faces of men, women and children killed by the *Dictadura*.

The blank frames? They were Suyai and JC, Cody and Ayelen. And the rest of the unknowns that were taken, like the men in Cambodia whose families never got a chance to say goodbye. Even as I went through the motions of my everyman life in the California hills, selling mini-mansions and trying to forget those faces, there was a space for them in Chile. Maybe they hadn't been counted, but at least they hadn't been forgotten. They are gone, but they can't be forgotten.

"This smog is driving me crazy," says the pudgy taxista with the patrician's coiffure of silver hair and the smooth baritone voice.

"You can hardly even see the mountains right now." He pauses for comedic effect. "Or the pretty girls walking down the street."

"I don't remember it being this thick," I say. "It seems to have gotten worse." He doesn't know that I haven't seen Santiago since the *Golpe*, but I withhold that thought.

The taxi is bending its way through the Providencia neighborhood on the way to the national soccer stadium. A swarm of fans waving red and blue flags surrounds us, circulating through the crawling traffic and pounding car hoods to punctuate their passionate singing.

"Where are you from?" the driver asks.

"Santiago, originally. But I've lived in the US for a while."

"Ah. America. What do you do there?"

I hesitate in answering, only because I am unsure what the true answer is. "Well, I've worked in real estate for most of my life."

He nods his head perfunctorily, a common reaction to the real-estate-as-profession response.

"But I am writing a book. A novel, actually."

"Really? Good for you. About what?" The automatic follow up question, the one that makes most writers cringe.

"I'm still not really sure." I run my hand through thinning hair. "It's about someone who wishes that today wasn't today, and tomorrow wasn't tomorrow. Something like that."

"Good luck with that," the driver says graciously, turning his shoulders to make eye contact. He has kind eyes that soften a long serrated scar above his right eyebrow.

"It's never too late to say whatever it is you have to say," he adds.

A minute of silence passes before the driver clears his throat and glances back at me. "So how long has it been since you were in Chile?"

"A long time. 1973, actually."

"1973, you say…."

We pass a moving percussion line to the right, a procession of men with huge drums pounding out bass lines for the songs that La U's fans sing throughout the game. Although it is winter, the day is unseasonably warm and the men lugging the weighty drums are sweating noticeably, though they don't seem to mind. They drum and chant, the undisputed nerve center of this swelling mass that convenes on game days.

The taxi driver's voice snaps me back to the present. "Sir, should I drop you off on the west side of the stadium? That's where fans of La U enter. Are you a fan of La U? Are you a *Chuncho?*"

I consider the question for a moment, unpacking its levels like a Russian babushka doll, the deeper meanings unearthed only by cracking open the outer layers. Am I still who I was? Am I still loyal to my father? What remains of my love for Ayelen? What constitutes my loyalty to Hope?

"Yes, I suppose I am. I suppose I'll always be a *Chuncho.* You can drop me off at Avenida Maratón."

The traffic lurches forward, slowed by the fans, the mounted policemen and the innumerable taxis carrying Chileans to the most important game of the season. As the stadium rises into view, my friendly driver tenses noticeably.

"What about you, sir? Are you a *Chuncho?*" I ask him.

The driver exhales heavily. "Well, I used to be a fan of La U. But I haven't been to this stadium since I was a young man—since 1973."

In the rearview mirror I can see his face and I recognize the look in his eyes. I know it well, because I have seen it in my own mirror many times.

"Since the *Golpe,*" he says—"since then, I haven't been back. All the torture, the murders. Too much happened here. Too much has been forgiven, and forgotten. I can't do either."

We both remain quiet the rest of the ride, while skeletons from the past dance their jigs like macabre minstrels, reminding and reminiscing.

I leave the stadium after five minutes. Leaving has nothing to do with the game, or the rain starting to fall, or even the eardrum-pounding chants from the feuding *barras*. I leave because my presence at that stadium offers a pardon that I'm not ready to give.

As I descend the steps and cleave my way through the crowd, the cheers of young Chileans with spotless minds mock my sensitivity. I leave the stadium through a shadowy tunnel, weaving through a miasma of cigarette smoke and jostling bodies. With each block the roar of the stadium fades further into the background. After passing several more blocks, the stadium din vanishes completely. Thankfully, it again comes to seem less real.

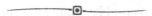

This book idea, I don't know where it's coming from or what's compelling me to do it. When I told Hope that I had begun writing a novel her reaction stopped me in my tracks.

"But you're just about the least imaginative person I know. How in the hell are you going to make up a whole novel?"

I didn't have a good answer for her. She was right about the imagination part. I admire creative people, musicians and poets and the like, but the most daring my imagination gets is when I order too-spicy food. There is a part of me that wonders if I'm seeking to create something profound to compensate for what life has become, a small-time real estate agent's standard-issue existence, interrupted only by prowling memories. This search to be profound—this driving need to be special or rich or famous and stand out from the crowd—strikes me as something afflicting my children's generation much more acutely than my own. I don't think I'm falling prey to self-indulgence, but we don't always see in ourselves what is obvious to outsiders.

The truth is, I have no illusions about my ability to invent a universe from scratch. That is to say, I am quite clear about my inability to do so. But I do have an advantage. I know beyond a shadow of a doubt that there are so many stories that deserve telling. There are men and women and children leading seemingly unexceptional lives that, upon closer examination, are operatic and heroic and tragic. They are people deserving of acknowledgement, stories far more profound than any work of fiction will ever be.

I may not be able to imagine a story, but as long as I'm walking around with a lifetime of memories ricocheting around my head, I might as well get it on paper. *A Dios regando y con el mazo dando.* My powder is dry, friends. My powder is dry.

To wit: I have disclosed that Suyai was disappeared after the *Golpe*, something Jorge told me before he too was disappeared. It was only years later, after my father died, that I summoned the nerve to write an old colleague of his who had risen to a prominent position in the Chilean Army during the *Dictadura*. While the letter was slightly misleading—I said that my father's dying wish had been to learn what became of his sister-in-law—it was my only chance to get more information. In the letter I shared the information that Jorge had sent in his last letter, when he revealed that Suyai had been imprisoned on a Navy ship following the *Golpe*. And that she never came back.

The General wrote back a few weeks later.

> *Benjamin,*
>
> *I have no knowledge of the event in question and will deny any knowledge of this correspondence if necessary. But your father was a friend and I sympathize with your family's search.*
>
> *I have looked into the matter. Suffice to say that the original information you received is correct.*
>
> *I am sorry for your loss.*
>
> *Cordially,*
> *General Pizarro*

A year after I received the General's letter, Chile released the official report documenting the abuses committed during and after the *Golpe*. The report cited the use of a giant four-masted navy vessel innocuously named the *Esmeralda* as a floating prison where female political prisoners were held after the *Golpe*. The report stated that this particular ship was used for the interrogation, rape and murder of female prisoners. Suyai, a woman too poor to have ever been on a boat in her life, spent her last days imprisoned on a very opulent one.

I have often wondered about the men on that naval ship. I've wondered what went through their minds when they gagged and unceremoniously dumped women into vats of piss and feces with their hands and feet bound together. I've wondered what they thought about as they beat them with cold wooden truncheons and attached alligator clips to their breasts and genitalia to send electricity coursing through their bodies. And I've wondered what they said when they arrived home to their wives and children after work and were asked, *Daddy, how was your day?* Was it just another day at the office for them? Was it anything out of the ordinary, their nine to five of rape and torture and murder? I wonder about these things, and I wonder what craven depths men are capable of. And then I realize that I don't really know much at all.

To say that the trip was entirely spur of the moment isn't being completely honest. While I only bought the plane ticket at the last minute, I've been thinking about this return since Pinochet died. Although the *Dictadura* ended two decades ago I couldn't go back until the man was dead. Irrational as it is, there was a lingering fear that despite all its progress Chile could never be safe while he was alive. Someday I want my family to see this part of their heritage, but I needed to go alone first. I needed to see it with my own eyes, to make sure that bringing them wouldn't expose them to a past that I've never been able to share with them.

The main reason I've wanted to go is to find out what happened to Salvador. Based on Jorge's last letter I believed that Salvador had been disappeared along with Suyai, or sent away into orphaned exile, to Peru or Brazil or some other country with a sympathetic military regime—the Chilean secret service didn't get too wrapped up in something as trifling as age in the hunt for Allende sympathizers. But after Jorge disappeared, I had no way to contact anyone in Chile to confirm the news. I never knew for sure, though, and over the years I've never stopped wondering if there wasn't some way he was alive, hoping for some implausible turn of fate that spared him. What's more, I had no idea how to find him. But there was always a chance.

The Internet revealed nothing, the phone book less. The City of Santiago and the Municipality of Ñuñoa also had no information; not only did they not have a current address, there is no record of Salvador ever existing. It made me wonder about the mischief that must have taken place when the Junta decided to kill someone, of the disappearances of birth certificates, marriage licenses and the like—the erasing of someone's official mark on the world.

The only option left is to go looking for my cousin.

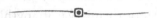

Ñuñoa is a different world from the barrio of dilapidated bungalows and corner stores that I recall from my youth. The streets are lined with cherry trees and the houses are framed by ornate metal gates and orderly shrubs. Behind the gates and painted adobe walls, tidy middle class homes repose on manicured lawns. It looks like a nice place to live, friendlier and less garish than the desiccated gated communities of California.

Lacking other options, I've come to Suyai's old house looking for a miracle. The road in front of Suyai's old lot is now paved and newly laid sidewalks line the street. Passing by this familiar street pulls me back to that winter when I was a young man and returned to Chile. But I can't let that digression happen, not yet. I can't lose myself in the past before first learning the truth.

In the place where her home once stood is a comfortable two-story suburban house with a glossy red door. I pass through the front yard and knock quietly. After a few moments, a middle-aged woman opens the heavy door a crack, just enough to see outside.

"Hello?"

"Hi, my name is Benjamin Piñera. I am looking for information about relatives who used to live here. Their names were Cristián and Suyai Contreras. They had a young boy named Salvador."

"I'm sorry, we only moved in a few years ago. This house has been bought and sold many times since it was built."

I wait a moment, hoping she volunteers more information, but she pulls back from the doorway.

"Thank you," I say, and retrace my steps through the yard. As I near the street she calls out to me.

"But you could ask the old woman in the blue house on the corner. She has lived in this neighborhood all her life."

From the street, the blue house appears empty. The marigold curtains are pulled tight over the front windows. The lawn is overgrown and weeds cover the front walk.

I knock a few times but hear nothing. As I begin to leave, the door slowly creaks open and a little old lady peeks her head outside.

"Can I help you?" The voice is shaky, but her eyes are clear and kind.

"Yes, ma'am. I am looking for information about family members who used to live down the street named Cristián and Suyai Contreras. They had a young boy, Salvador."

The woman's face lights up at the mention of their names. "Yes, of course. I remember Suyai and Salvador well. You do know about Cristián, don't you?"

"Yes, ma'am. My family lived in Chile until '70, and I returned for a short time in '73."

"Well, let's see. Suyai moved shortly before the *Golpe*, right? I'm sorry, but I haven't heard anything about her since. She never came back."

It seems that what I suspected all those years is true, that both Suyai and Salvador were killed. I thank her and start to say goodbye, but as I'm leaving she remembers something.

"But I think Salvador lives in Providencia. I heard he and his family live next to a gringo bar called California Picá."

I thank the old woman as I leave, one more link in a chain of undeserved kindness, and hail the first cab that passes, headed to a bar that shares a name with my old escape route.

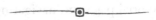

The cab drops me off in front of a dive bar with huge flat-screen televisions hanging prominently on the walls, offering patrons an authentic slice of Americana. Next door is a brick townhouse with toys strewn across the patio. As I approach I can hear children playing in the house, the warbling of squeaky voices and the pitter-patter of scurrying feet leaking out of the house. I take a deep breath and knock, steeling myself for one of the hardest conversations of my life.

A pretty woman in her early forties answers the door. She's wearing an apron and the harried smile of a mother with young children, with one eye on the task at hand and the other waiting for the imminent sound of something gone wrong.

"Good afternoon. What can I do for you?"

"Good afternoon. Is this the home of Salvador Contreras?"

"Yes, it is." As she answers her body subtly draws back behind the door.

"Is Salvador here right now? I would really like to talk to him."

"He'll be getting home from work very soon." The comment is offered as a fact as well as a warning. I remind myself that I am still a strange man at her door.

"Who are you and how do you know my husband?" she asks.

"It's a long story." I am unsure how to explain or where to start, so I blurt out the piece of information that seems most relevant.

"I'm Salvador's cousin, Benjamin. I didn't know he was alive until now. I don't know if he knows that I am alive either."

The color drains from her face. "Please, come in," she says, her voice quivering. "Salvador will be home from the newspaper soon."

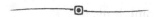

Salvador works as the managing editor at *El Mercurio*. In this role, he's second-in-command at the largest daily in Chile, a remarkable feat for someone from humble beginnings who was orphaned as a young a boy. What's even more remarkable, and jarring, is the bizarre symmetry of this news. My cousin holds the same position my father held for almost a decade, directing the editorial page and navigating tricky political waters for the paper.

I'm sitting on the couch when Salvador arrives. The minute he gets home, three screeching little girls race to the door and hug his legs, the youngest reaching around his knee and squeezing as hard as she can. Daniela, his wife, waits behind the girls as they welcome their dad home. He is handsome, with wavy dark hair and a proud chin. He looks like his father.

"Daddy! Daddy!" they scream as they pull him inside. As he steps into the house from the foyer, he sees me on the couch and shoots his wife a concerned look.

"*¿Quién es él?*" he asks warily.

"*Está bien,*" she says. "*Es familia.*"

Salvador's wife herds the girls into the kitchen and motions for him to join me in the living room. Salvador takes a few steps toward me, tosses his suit jacket on the back of a chair and sits down. His eyes remain fixed on me.

"Is it you, Benjamin? Is it really you?"

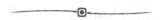

Sitting in their living room lined with family pictures, toys and children's books, it reminds me of our house in California when the kids were little, messy and bustling with the unbridled energy of small children. While Salvador talks quietly with his wife in the kitchen, I think about what to say to him, my little cousin who is now a grown man, and clearly shocked at my presence. While I have always held out hope for this moment, I am surprised by the excitement and nervousness that accompany it—I had thought exhilaration was a feeling that had deserted me some time ago. What will be harder, though, are the questions that will inevitably come. Why didn't I return sooner? Why didn't I try harder to find him?

When he comes back, I start the conversation off on a less alarming note. "How long have you worked at *El Mercurio*?"

"I'm coming up on fifteen years. But I started my career at a smaller paper called *La Voz del Pueblo*." We speak in English and his command of the language is impeccable, with only a faint accent that must have been refined through extensive practice. We also speak it because the girls are circulating around the house and we wordlessly consent to the need to shield his girls from this. After all, we're both fathers. Being a parent helps you understand things about the world on a different level, one that often removes yourself from consideration.

"It's hard to believe that you have the same job that my father did—you know that, right? That he was managing editor of *El Mercurio* from '62 to '70?"

"I do. It is pretty amazing. We obviously took very different paths to get there, though." As he loosens his tie and runs his hands through his hair, I see Suyai in him—in the strength of his visage, in his kind eyes and in the purposeful way he moves.

"But I'm proud to say that the newspaper has changed," he adds. "Sure, it still has its political leanings, but it's different than it was during the *Dictadura*."

"What's even harder to believe," I say, "is that I worked at *La Voz del Pueblo* too. I don't know if you remember that. You were so young then. Do you remember any of it?"

"When you were in Chile? I didn't know you worked there. That is incredible." He leans forward, closing the space between us, and in his face I recognize the little boy from so many years ago.

"I do have a few cloudy memories of you and your brother. He's your twin, right? I also vaguely recall meeting your friend, the tall one. Do they both live in California too?"

Outside, a gust of wind is buffeting a cherry tree in the front yard. It looks like it will start raining soon. As I look out the front window at the swaying branches and the darkening clouds, I choke down the emotions curdling in my stomach and turn my eyes back to Salvador.

"JC and Cody were killed in Santiago on September 11, 1973, the night of the *Golpe*. That was the night before I fled Chile. Salvador, there is so much we need to talk about—so much that has happened. Why don't we start at the beginning."

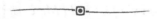

"Do you know what happened to your mother?"

Salvador takes a breath and considers how much to trust in me, this resurrected cousin appearing on his doorstep after decades away.

"I've spent all my life trying to learn what happened to her. Are you familiar with the Valech Report?"

"I read that report cover to cover looking for your names."

"So you know that she's not among the official victims—that they still consider her to be missing?"

"I do. After I left Chile I exchanged letters with Jorge until he disappeared. In his last letter he said you and your mother had been taken by the military. He also relayed a rumor that both of you had been killed, but I know that he was still looking for you."

Salvador smiles sadly. "I have good memories of that man. He did everything he could for us."

"Yes, he did. He also helped JC, Cody and I when we first arrived in Chile. And he helped me escape…."

We sit in momentary silence, two grown men revisiting a world unrecognizable from that of today.

"Salvador, you still don't know what happened to your mom, do you?

The years of unknowing heartbreak are etched in his face. "No, not for certain. I tell myself that she must have been killed because she would have come back for me if she was alive. But you always want to hope, don't you? Even though you know that hoping makes the hurt last. Somewhere deep down, I still hope."

I take a deep breath and measure my words. "I have something to tell you. I should have come to find you earlier. I'm sorry I didn't. Truly sorry, more than you'll ever know."

The look on his face only amplifies the guilt I feel for my cowardice, but he says nothing.

"I kept wondering about Suyai too. We loved her very much, and she took us in when my father refused us." I pause, gathering courage for the admission.

"A few years ago I contacted an old colleague of my father, a general in the Chilean Army. In the letter I asked if he could confirm the last piece of information Jorge sent before he disappeared. Jorge said your mom had been taken to a boat in the port of Valparaiso where female prisoners were interrogated."

"And what did this general say?"

"Without saying it directly—well, he made it clear that your mom had been taken there. And that she never made it out."

Salvador's face is one of a boy who has lost his mother. There is no silver lining in this. It is loss, plain and simple, the deepest kind that exists.

"I guess I could be angry at you," he finally says. "But I'm not. Now that I know—well, now that I know she's gone, I can't really keep hoping, can I?"

"I am sorry. I should have come earlier. I just couldn't come back."

I know full well the shortcomings of my explanation, my fear of coming back a paltry justification.

Salvador stands up and walks toward the kitchen. "Would you like a drink? I need a scotch."

"Yeah. Whatever you're having, on the rocks."

Salvador returns a few minutes later with two clinking tumblers.

"You have a beautiful family," I say. "How old are your girls?"

"Josefina is 7, Karina is 5 and Suyai just turned 3."

"They're adorable. They all look like their mother."

"Thank goodness," he says. "They are wonderful, aren't they? Growing up in orphanages, I always wondered if I would have a family someday. It was the only thing I ever remember wanting. This may sound strange, but even after what happened I feel blessed."

My cousin is right. There is always something that remains, replete with the heartbreak and loss, but blessed all the same.

"So, tell me about life in California. Disgustingly rich like all the rest of them?"

"You know it. Everybody's a millionaire in America, aren't they?" We share a sardonic laugh.

"Naw. Comfortable, but not rich."

"Married? Kids?"

"Married, three kids. My wife's name is Hope and we've been married thirty-two years. We have three kids. Thomas is twenty-eight. He and his wife live near us on the Central Coast, and they have a baby boy, Juan Carlos. Nathan is twenty-five, and off gallivanting through Europe somewhere right now. He's a screenwriter, and plans to move to Hollywood when he gets back. And then there's Maribel, my little girl. My pride and joy. She just finished her degree at Stanford and is moving to San Francisco in a month. She's staying with us in the meantime."

"So, all in all, a big happy family?" he asks.

Salvador's comment catches me off guard. My surprise at his reaction to a simple run-down of the what and where of my family suddenly seems ridiculous.

"I suppose it is, all things considered."

Why am I surprised that the life Hope and I have built sounds like a good one? I realize now that I shouldn't be. Despite everything that's happened, and despite those skeletons that dance their midnight waltz and probably always will, we haven't done so badly after all. I haven't done so badly after all.

I join Salvador and his family for dinner and dessert, empanadas followed by a sumptuous *torta de tres leches* that Daniela whips up for the occasion, and then play with the girls after dinner. At first they are hesitant, but Daniela pulls them aside and tells them that I'm their uncle, that I'm part of the family. Soon they warm up and begin to show me their books and their dolls, and they beg me to give them plane rides through the air. Their darling little voices call me Uncle Benjamin. It is the happiest I've been since Maribel was born twenty-three years ago.

After the girls go upstairs to get ready for bed, I talk to Salvador about bringing the family to Chile to visit. My flight is scheduled to leave tomorrow, but I've decided to postpone my return a few days. I want to stop by and see them again and make the most of this precious time.

It's getting late when I say goodnight. Daniela and the girls give me hugs before I leave. The girls' attempts to wrap their little arms around my big belly are comical, and break my heart. As Salvador walks me out to Avenida Providencia to find a cab, we weave through swarms of breezy barhopping youths, yelling and laughing in the lightness of youth, like young people deserve. A cab pulls up beside me and Salvador gives me a hug. As I turn to get in the cab, he pulls me back.

"Remember, no matter what has happened, we are family. We are survivors."

We are survivors. We are family.

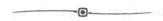

As for the letter from *El Museo de la Memoria,* the second thing that I couldn't forget, it was written by a thirty-three year-old husband and father. As he was waiting for the military to arrest him the day of the *Golpe* he wrote a letter to his wife, and one to his children.

Niñitos:

> *Behave yourselves well and eat all of your food. Study hard and help your mom around the house.*
>
> *I don't know when I'll be home to see you again. Don't watch too much television and behave yourselves like the good kids you are.*
>
> *Goodbye, and don't forget your daddy.*
>
> *I wish you happiness.*
> *Littré Quiroga C.*

Mr. Quiroga had been a government employee in the Allende administration. He was arrested on September 11, 1973 by the Military Junta. His bullet-riddled body was found on September 16, 1973 outside of Cementerio Metropolitano along with the bodies of five other victims.

Those that were taken, where would they be now?

Cody would be living somewhere near Bakersfield, working as a construction foreman. (I always saw him leading a construction crew, a humble leader of men, just like in Vietnam.) He would be married, with a satchel of kids running wild in the Valley and wreaking havoc on the Central Coast beaches. He would drive a massive tricked-out pickup truck, give his buddies rides to work and faithfully attend his kids' football games and parent teacher conferences. He would be a good man, just like he always was, a husband and father and friend.

Suyai would be the same as she always was, a doting mom and grandma with a feisty streak, shouting at the top of her lungs at political rallies and unapologetically waving the Allende flag. She would have loved post-Pinochet Chile, with its impromptu protests, raucous public debates and bold opinions. And she would have loved speaking her mind without fearing that someone would come knocking at her door in the middle of the night. She would be the same benevolent force, a powerful and loving person with a heart of gold. But she would have had another lifetime to share it.

I like to think that Ayelen and I would be living in a little wood cabin on Rio Baker, deep in the heart of Patagonian Chile, with a few boys running around that would look a lot like JC and me. I would take the boys out to fish when dusk settled in, just as the trout began to feed, and teach them the quiet secrets of the river. Ayelen would make a fire and cook the fish that we caught. After dinner, I would tuck the kids into bed, throw a few logs on the fire and then head to our room where I would kiss Ayelen goodnight and reach for her hand in the middle of the bed. We would fall asleep, interlocked and inseparable. This would be my life.

And my brother? JC would have married a Chilean girl—I am as sure of it as I am that the sun will rise tomorrow—and settled somewhere on the Central Coast for a while, in a quiet little house with a couple kids of his own. After the *Dictadura* ended, he probably would have moved his family back to Chile. He would have been a strict father but a good one, I like to think, a blend of Father's obduracy and Mother's warmth. The excesses would have been tempered by a better life, one bereft of the disappointments inflicted upon Dad.

Dad. How strange the word sounds, a dissonant tone in a foreign language. How I wish it weren't just a relic from a long-ago childhood.

I miss them not for what could have been for me but for what never was for them. I have missed them for almost forty years. I miss them in my dreams, and I miss them right now, in these very seconds that pass by. I will miss them always, and I will never forget them. Not again.

THE END

Publication permission graciously offered courtesy of the Quiroga family